Childhood

ALSO BY ANDRÉ ALEXIS

Despair and Other Stories of Ottawa

Childhood

A NOVEL

André Alexis

HENRY HOLT AND COMPANY   •   NEW YORK

Henry Holt and Company, Inc.
Publishers since 1866
115 West 18th Street
New York, New York 10011

Henry Holt ® is a registered trademark of
Henry Holt and Company, Inc.

Library of Congress Cataloging-in-Publication Data
Alexis, André, 1957–
Childhood: a novel / André Alexis. — 1st American ed.
p.   cm.
ISBN 0-8050-5981-4 (hardcover: alk. paper)
I. Title.
PR9199.3.A365C45   1998
813′.54—dc 21   98-13089

Henry Holt books are available for special promotions
and premiums. For details contact: Director, Special Markets.

First American Edition 1998

Designed by Kelly Soong

Printed in the United States of America
All first editions are printed on acid-free paper. ∞

1   3   5   7   9   10   8   6   4   2

To   Thecla Kathleen
           Michele Lise
           Denise Ann

And

           Horace Clayton Alexis

Quels livres as-tu lus,
en dehors de ceux qui conservent la voix des femmes
et des choses irréelles?

. . .

Et les livres que tu écris
bruiront de choses irréelles—
irréelles à force de trop être,
comme les songes.

What books have you read,
besides those that preserve the voices of women
and things unreal?

. . .

And the books you write
will rustle with things unreal—
unreal because too real,
like dreams.

— JEAN-JOSEPH RABEARIVELO

History

I

It has been six months since my mother died; a shade less since Henry passed. In that time, I've stayed home and I've kept things tidy.

They have been much on my mind.

I've been thinking about Love, you see, and theirs was the first and most puzzling romance I witnessed. I didn't understand it at the time. I still find it odd, though now it also seems a sad thing to contemplate.

Contemplate it I will, though, or contemplate it I must.

I've decided to write, to do something between housecleaning and the dreams I have about your shoulders.

Not that I'm idle.

I do a great deal of reading and some cooking. Besides, you'd be surprised how much there is to be done in or around a room. It's far from dull, I can tell you, but diversion depends on discipline. You have to break the day into manageable portions, and that takes a clock and a little resolve.

It takes a timetable:

> 7 o'clock: I am awakened by the alarm.
> 8 o'clock: I clean my bedroom.

9 o'clock:	I feed Alexander (seed).
10 o'clock:	I read poetry.
11 o'clock:	I continue to read poetry.
12 o'clock:	I prepare my meal of the day. I eat it.
1 o'clock (P.M.):	I write letters (to the *Citizen*).
2 o'clock (P.M.):	I clean my bedroom.
3 o'clock (P.M.):	I prepare tea.
4 o'clock (P.M.):	I set out for a walk, and walk with you in mind. (We've known each other for over a year now.)
5 o'clock (P.M.):	I read the newspaper.
6 o'clock (P.M.):	I read philosophy.
7 o'clock (P.M.):	I continue to read.
8 o'clock (P.M.):	I meditate on what I've read.
9 o'clock (P.M.):	I feed Alexander (fruit, vegetables).
10 o'clock (P.M.):	I bathe.
11 o'clock (P.M.):	I prepare the next day's schedule.
12 (A.M.) to 6 (A.M.):	Sleep.

Of course, this gives you no idea of the wealth of my existence. It doesn't take me an hour to wake from sleep. Nor does it take me an hour to feed Alexander. I can make tea in fifteen minutes, and there are days when I have no letters to write. I don't confine myself to the reading of poetry or philosophy, and, although I do clean the bedroom twice a day, there are a number of ways to go about it, each with its own appeal.

Still, none of this gives me the focus I'd like. I brood. I often brood.

Perhaps writing is the discipline I need.

So I will write, precisely, about my mother and Henry, about Love, with you in mind, from the beginning.

———

I had a singular childhood.

My parents went their separate ways at my birth and I was sent to live with my grandmother.

My grandmother, *Mrs.* Edna MacMillan, lived in Petrolia.

I don't think she was pleased to have me. She was past the age of easy tolerance, and she was cantankerous. (When I was five or six, I went through a phase about God making mountains He himself couldn't lift, until my grandmother told me that He didn't exist, so there was no use, my going on about it.)

Also, she used to drink a lot of dandelion wine. And, from the time I could tell a dandelion from a thistle, she sent me out to cull them from lawns and fields all over the neighborhood.[1]

She wasn't a cruel woman, but she was erratic. You couldn't always tell where you stood with her. At least, I couldn't. And her only loves were the wine she made and the poetry of Archibald Lampman:

> *From plains that reel to southward, dim,*
> *The road runs by me white and bare;*
> *Up the steep hill it seems to swim*
> *Beyond, and melt into the glare . . .*

---

[1] In summer, the field across the street from our house was yellow with dandelions and spiky with thistles. It smelled of weeds and pine.

Along with a basket for the dandelions, I'd take a glass jar with me, to catch grasshoppers and crickets. In fact, quite a bit of my time was taken up with insects: finding them, catching them, admiring their wings and antennae before setting them free.

And so on . . .

It was a strange combination, wine and Lampman, but I once used the poetry against the wine, so I was grateful for it.

My grandmother was sixty-five years old when I was abandoned to her care, a retired schoolteacher, thin as a compass, with an aureole of white hair. Her eyes were liver brown, and her nose was slightly bent to one side of her face.

Outwardly, she was predictable. She usually wore one of two dresses: there was a long, short-sleeved summer dress with red and black flowers on a white background, and there was a long-sleeved winter dress with red and white flowers on a black background. She woke at seven o'clock every morning, and she drank a small tumbler of wine. If she'd had a bad night, she would drink two.

Perhaps, in the distant past, this steadied her nerves, but, when I knew her, the wine didn't help at all.

When she was really depressed, there was no telling what breakfast would be like. I had Pablum for breakfast until I was seven years old, so the Pablum was a sure thing. Sometimes she fed me herself. Sometimes she put a bowl of Pablum before me. Sometimes she gave me a spoon, sometimes a fork. And once, in a fit of giddiness, she used her wooden spoon as a catapult and fired the warm Pablum at me from the pot.

Much of how the day turned out was determined by breakfast.

I'm not saying I was abused, but there were times when she'd hit me pretty hard with her wooden spoon, and times when she'd hit me with whatever was nearby. (I don't know if anyone else has been punished with an eggbeater, but I was, once.) I can't always remember why she hit me. There wasn't always a good reason, but the time I'm thinking of, when I used her beloved Lampman against her, was one of those when I'd done something wrong.

I'd fallen in the field across from our house and cut my hand on a broken mason jar. Instead of asking for a bandage, as I should have, I'd gone to get one for myself. The bandages were on the lower shelf of the bathroom cabinet, and I could just reach them if I stood on my toes. What I did, though, was knock over a bottle of iodine. It shattered in the sink. My grandmother came to see what was going on.

I was six or seven at the time, no match for her. She had been drinking, and she had a frying pan with her. I saw it rise above me. I put up my hands to protect my head. I don't know what inspired me to recite poetry, but I did:

> *Now hath the summer reached her golden close,*
> *And, lost amid her cornfields, bright of soul,*
> *Scarcely perceives from her divine repose*
> *How near, how swift, the inevitable goal . . .*

There I was, hands raised up, squeaking out the first verse of "September," the only Lampman I knew by heart, having heard it from her hundreds of times.

And the poem smoothed her out.

— Clever monkey, she said

walking unsteadily back to the kitchen and her kitchenware.

It all seems improbable now, and yet I remember every word of the poem. The incident is all the more remarkable in that, at that age, I couldn't have understood much of Lampman's meaning.

Petrolia wasn't very interesting. I can say that now, having other places to compare it to. I suppose it was a fine environment for a child, though. There was a good deal of nature: the earth, mice, frogs, insects, the froth of spawning carp, turtles, and birds.

The town was cold and white in winter. It was wet in spring, warm in summer, and cold again in autumn; just what you'd expect from Southern Ontario. There were few people, and fewer buildings. There was a golf course, a tile factory, a dam. And in spring, when the only river in town overflowed, it usually managed to take a small child with it.

My friends at the time, I mean when I was five or six, were Sandy Berwick, the Goodman sisters, and the Schwartzes, all of whom lived close by.

Sandy's backyard abutted ours. His father was Reverend Berwick. We were friends because I was the only child who could stand him.

Our first meeting went something like this:

I was in the garden pulling weeds. From his side of the fence, Sandy said

— My name's Berwick . . . What're you doing?

— Picking weeds.

— For Mrs. MacMillan?

— For my grandmother.

— She's very old . . .

— Yes, she's pretty old.

— Is she Christian?

— I don't think so.

— Ohh . . . that's awful . . .

He walked away. He was wearing shorts and white socks that went up to his knees. He came back a minute later.

— She has to be converted, you know, he said.

Then he walked off again.

I had no idea what he was talking about, but it seemed significant. He had things in line. My grandmother was old. She wasn't Christian. She had to be converted.

The Goodmans were our neighbors on one side; the Schwartzes were on the other.

There were three Goodman sisters: Jane, Andrea, and Margaret. They all had pixie cuts, which Mrs. Goodman gave them the first Friday of every month. The three sisters were popular. There were usually half a dozen girls in the Goodmans' backyard every day until five o'clock, and when they weren't in the yard, they were in the basement playing with dolls or listening to records on their portable record player.

The Goodmans' basement was fascinating to me. The walls were paneled with slats that smelled of pine. Near the foot of the stairs there was a bar. Its counter was white arborite. Behind it were shelves of brightly colored bottles. There were also mysterious gadgets: a piggy bank in the shape of a woman in a bathing suit, a bottle opener like a Lilliputian golf club, a mug with flesh-colored breasts jutting from it, and plastic ice cubes with flies in them. Here and there, tacked to the wall, there were postcards from Florida and snapshots of Mr. and Mrs. Goodman on vacation.

The basement was carpeted. There were easy chairs and an upholstered sofa. In a separate room, there was a Ping-Pong table. It all seemed so luxurious, so wealthy.

In contrast, our basement was a dark and mildewed punishment.

I didn't go to the Goodmans' often, because I was shy and because Mr. Goodman didn't like me, but it was at the Goodmans' that I learned to skip rope, to turn double Dutch and Irish, to tell the difference between a doll in summer clothes and a doll in sportswear, to make papier-mâché heads and construction-paper silhouettes.

And, as it happens, Margaret Goodman was my first love.

On the other side, the Schwartzes lived in a redbrick two-story house that was the smallest on Grove Street. It was also the most beautiful. The house was covered in ivy, and the property penned by an unruly hedge. In the front windows, one on either side of the door, there were white flower boxes which, in spring, were filled with tulips.

When I knew them, Mrs. Schwartz was twenty-five and her daughter, Irene, was five.

As far as I remember, Lillian Schwartz was the only person who ever talked about my mother: my mother as a child, the dolls she liked, the books she read, the park on King where she fell from the seesaw; my mother adolescent, beautiful in certain dresses, squabbling with her parents; and then her sudden departure, at the age of seventeen, with a man from Sarnia.

In Lillian Schwartz's version of her, I discerned something of myself. I imagined my mother thin, shy, and unhappy.

Also, Mrs. Schwartz never spoke down to me. She behaved as if I were a colleague. When she took a correspondence course on religion, for instance, I was pushed into the frightening universe of charmed weeds, dying saints, and the restless dead.

To this day I can't think of Philo of Alexandria without a shudder, but Lillian Schwartz was the adult I loved most, after my grandmother, and she was more trustworthy, in my eyes.

II

Now that I've known so many unhappy people, I understand my grandmother's misery.

She had lived something other than the life she wanted. She had married late, then her husband left her. (He died, actually, but she held it against him, I think.)

For years she had taught primary school, though she had no fondness for children, and she had whelped, if that's the word, an ungrateful child. After a life like that, passed in a town so far from the world, what was there to do but subside in drink and wait for her pension checks?

Then I was forced on her.

She could have drowned me, poisoned me, left me in traffic, or fed me to wild dogs—all of which she threatened to do. Instead, in her own way, she sheltered me. (There is even, at the edge of memory, a memory of sleep in her arms; her sour smell, her dry white hair . . .)

I didn't understand how much each kindness to me cost her. To feed and clothe a child who, on top of everything else, resembled her reckless daughter. Imagine.

And then there were her friends, the two or three old ladies who visited from time to time. They smelled of baby powder and dirty clothes. They held my chin in their hands and shook my face until I was dizzy, and then said things like

— He looks just like Katarina . . .

— It doesn't look like you're taking care of him, Eddy . . .

— He's a little animal . . .

— I don't think you're raising him right . . .

and shook my face some more.

That must have rubbed salt in the wound.

So, my survival was a fortuitous thing. As soon as I learned to, I steered clear of my grandmother. The less she saw of me, the more tolerable I was.

Now, as I mentioned, I met Sandy Berwick while I was pulling weeds from the garden.

His idea that my grandmother had to be converted was still a little beyond comprehension. Religious conversion wasn't, until Mrs. Schwartz began her studies, an issue for me. As far as I could tell, we—my grandmother and I—were not religious at all. It was she who told me God did not exist, and we rarely saw the inside of a church together.

Obviously, Sandy's upbringing was different from my own. His father was a minister of the United Church. His family was devout, but I don't think that explains his fervor. His mind had latched on to an idea and it would not let go.

Sometime after our first meeting, I was in the backyard again. It was a hot day. The garden was parched. (We called it a garden, but there were no flowers to speak of, only a row of sunflowers that drooped in our direction, though they belonged to the Berwicks.) I had found a stick with which I could poke holes in the ground, and I had discovered an anthill.

This time I saw Sandy coming before he spoke to me.

— You want to be friends? he asked.

— I don't mind.

— What're you doing?

— Digging holes.

— What for?

— I don't know.

— You want to see my house?

— Sure.

I was obsessed with other people's houses. I remember the Berwicks' house in its particulars. It smelled clean. It was ethereal in its cleanliness.

The stairs to the second floor were carpeted. The kitchen was spotless: no Pablum stains, no greasy tiles, no signs of violence. The furniture, what little there was, was all straight lines. (Though other houses were more inviting, the Berwicks' was where I would have chosen to live.)

Mrs. Berwick met us as soon as we entered.

— Te voilà, Alexandre, she said, kissing Sandy's ears. Tu as un ami? Tu me le présente?

She held him close, smiling politely as we were introduced, pleased her son had found a friend.

— Tu veux quelque chose à manger, chéri? Ça fait déjà deux heures depuis déjeuner. Tu n'as pas faim? Oui, tu as sûrement faim. Viens manger un peu.

She led us to the kitchen table and put a basket of oranges before us. She cut two slices of cake (canary yellow, impossibly sweet) and put them on small plates. She brought us glasses of milk.

Sandy wasn't interested. He watched me eat, without touching his food. His mother tried everything to encourage him. She stood behind him and played with his hair. She whispered to him. She nibbled on the cake herself, until, at last, he broke a corner from the slice and put it on the tip of his tongue.

— Tu vois? she said. Miam miam . . .

I was confused. My grandmother never fussed over what I ate, and I ate whatever was before me.

When we were finished, Mrs. Berwick inspected Sandy's plate. He had eaten enough to satisfy her (half the cake, a section of orange), so she let us go.

Sandy's room was much like the rest of the house. It was carpeted. It smelled of nothing in particular. The walls were white. There was a neatly made bed, above which hung a painting of Christ surrounded by young children.

And there were short bookshelves, filled with books in French.[2]

On top of one of the shelves, Sandy had a cage of white rats, two of them: Aline and Pierre.

---

[2] I don't know how it had been for him, but I had been reading since the age of four. And learning to read, as with most of what my grandmother taught me, had been traumatic.

She'd started me in on the alphabet from the time I could say "gramaw." There had been hours at the kitchen table: I, small and nervous, on one side, my grandmother, armed with cards and a yardstick, on the other. You can believe I learned the letters quickly.

— Put your hand on the table. Now, what's this?

— A?

— That's right. And this?

— D?

Smack! A rap across the knuckles.

— Are you guessing?

The clean house, the tidy room, the neat backyard. By and large, they were the borders of Sandy's world.

He would have preferred to play baseball, to swim in the water hazard at the golf course, to throw stones at passing cars, but with his asthma there wasn't much chance of that. Whenever he ran for more than a few steps, he would collapse, breathless, and I would have to help him with his inhaler, or wait until he recovered.

We didn't do much together. We read our comics, occasionally explored the woods behind the tile factory, or disposed of

---

— O?

Smack! Another rap across the knuckles.

— Don't guess. What is it?

— It's D.

— That's right. And this . . . ?

From the letters themselves we turned to their sounds. That was even more obscure. How was it that "A" could be

"A" as in f<u>a</u>ther

"A" as in m<u>a</u>ke

"A" as in h<u>a</u>ve.

What were the rules?

Nor did my grandmother limit herself to short words when it came to pronunciation. For every "bake" there was a "prestidigitate," a "necromancy," or a "maneuver." Difficult words indeed, but I learned to pronounce them, and she never broke any of my fingers.

Then we began to read.

It would have been nice to have simpler things, like *Mother Goose Rhymes* or *Struwwelpeter*. Instead, we read English poetry and Dickens, boatloads of Dickens.

To be fair, it was something of a pleasure meeting English this way, but once I'd gained confidence, she started in on French. I learned that language the same way, though I speak it with a Trinidadian accent.

the rats born to Aline and Pierre. Somehow, that was enough to kill the hours between breakfast and supper (in summer) or afternoon and evening (during the school year).

It wasn't an enduring friendship. The Berwicks moved to Wyoming when I was eight, and there was no good-bye.

The things I most remember about Sandy are his desire to convert my grandmother, his trouble breathing, his clean home, and his mother's body.

When we'd been friends for two years, Sandy went through a phase.

It began when we discovered a stack of rude magazines in the woods behind the tile factory.

The tile factory was abandoned and decrepit. It was just past the golf course on the edge of town, within walking distance of our homes. (That is, Sandy could walk to it without suffering.) Behind the factory was a tract of bush, thistles, and thin trees. A shallow stream ran through it, and it was a perfect place for catching grasshoppers, field mice, shrews, and frogs.

In the middle of all this scrub, there was a shack, a lean-to really, only big enough to accommodate half a dozen children at a time. It was a foul-smelling place on the inside, and it was, in its way, dangerous. We felt courageous exploring it.

The magazines were inside the shack.

They were, most of them, "gentlemen's" magazines, full of color photographs of naked women. Two of them, however, were mystifying.

The first, *My Darling Horse*, had photographs of a woman with her hand on a horse's penis or with her mouth around it.

(In one instance, she was hanging on to the horse's body with its penis inside her.)

The second had no cover at all. It was full of pictures of men and women burning each other. They were naked, but they weren't otherwise engaged. They simply burned each other with cigarettes and butane lighters, candles and cigars. That was it.

These two we thought too awful to keep, so we left them where they were. The others we took with us to a new hiding place. We buried them at the foot of a birch tree beside the factory. And we returned to the magazines every so often until they disintegrated.[3]

Their effect on Sandy was immediate. Whereas before we had wandered around the woods and fields talking about nothing in particular, we now talked of nothing but women. Were they all like those in the magazines? Did they all have vaginas? What would it be like if they didn't? How would you know? Could you ask?

And then, one day, Sandy wondered aloud if his mother was "vaginaed" or not. I hadn't thought of Mrs. Berwick that way, but, to my mind, it was certain she was.

— Of course she has a vagina, I said.

---

[3] These magazines were my first proof that the adults around us were engaged in something obscure. It was also the first time I was aware of being sexually aroused, without knowing that that's what it was. I couldn't understand the horse or the burns, but most of the other images did something to me that translated, physically, as a racing heartbeat, a feeling of anxiety, and an unwanted, though not entirely disagreeable, forgive me for mentioning it, tumescence.

If I could choose, this would not have been my first sexual experience. It's annoying to be taken back to those woods, to the sound of birds, the smell of earth and trees, the stink of the cabin.

— How do you know?

After a long and thoughtful discussion, I had to admit I didn't. How could I? But why wouldn't Mrs. Berwick have one? We all had penises, didn't we? (Though, there too, the question was moot.)

I would have preferred to let the matter drop, but for Sandy it was a pretext. He began to plan the best way for the two of us to discover his mother's private province.

We spent more time at his house.

We hid in the bathroom for hours, waiting for his mother to come in.

— Mais qu'est-ce que vous faites dans la salle de bain?

He repeatedly asked if we could hide under her skirt.

— Mais pourquoi?

Whenever her hands were full, he would pull her dress up as high as he could.

— Alexandre! Laisse Maman tranquille!

We would hide in the bedroom closet with the door open just wide enough for us to see what was going on. (Once, this almost worked, but as Mrs. Berwick began to undress, Sandy giggled in anticipation and she found us out.)

The remarkable thing in all this was Mrs. Berwick's patience. It must have been obvious what we were after, but she was indulgent.

And, in fact, we finally did see her naked, but it wasn't as Sandy had planned.

One summer afternoon when we were being typically bothersome, Mrs. Berwick threw up her hands and said

— Bon. Aujourd'hui nous allons à la plage.

— That's a wonderful idea, said Reverend Berwick.

It didn't seem like a wonderful idea to us, but we helped her make ham sandwiches and lemonade, and we climbed into the car.

The ride was interminable.

We drove out of town, past Sarnia, past farm fields and farm animals and farmhouses, taking gravel roads and dirt roads. Then, when Reverend Berwick stopped the car, we walked along a pebbled path until we came to a small lake.

There were clouds in the sky, but the sun was shining. The water was clear and cold. The narrow beach smelled of the pine trees along the shore. The ground was a little stony, so we had to watch where we stepped. Reverend Berwick put two baby-blue beach towels down, and then he and Mrs. Berwick undressed. Just like that, neither casually nor self-consciously. Mrs. Berwick let down her hair and put her glasses in her husband's jacket.

— Vous vous déshabillez pas? she asked us.

Her body was pink and white. She had heavy breasts, their light-blue veins reticulated. Her nipples were dark and, yes, she had a vagina, or at least the pubic hair that suggested it. Reverend Berwick was thin. His body was white and soft-looking. Naturally, he had a penis.

They both went slowly into the water, and then Reverend Berwick plunged in.

Sandy and I reluctantly undressed and joined them. Sandy stayed in the shallow water by himself, but, once I got used to it, I went out as far as I could.

Now, of course, I understand what was memorable about all this. It wasn't the Berwicks' nakedness as such. They were as tidy with their clothes off as on. It was my awareness that they must always have been at ease with their bodies.

There was no doubt Sandy had seen his mother's body. He had plotted so that I should see it, and not like this, either. Our day at the beach was a disappointment to him. Why? Because I'm convinced he had his own reason for having me see his mother's body.

Perhaps he wished to embarrass her, or, again, perhaps he was proud to show me what he had already seen.

Whatever the case, his motive eludes me. To this day, I can't get it straight.

III

Two words forward, one word back. I'm surprised at how arduous it is to write. How arduous it is to arrange my own life.

I get up at seven as usual, but most of the day is filled with scribbling.

My timetables aren't all that helpful, but I'm wary of keeping too strictly to schedule. I mean, I'm comforted by things in place, but I've learned to temper my inclination.

My first timetable was an act of desperation. It was made in 1978. I was suffering through an episode. I was confused and tired. I'd spent three days staring at a dirty basement window.

And then a car horn sounded in the distance, somewhere along Gilmour Street. I heard it and, for no reason I can understand, I suddenly saw the moments in a day as if they were the beads on a chaplet.

It was transcendent.

I wrote my first entry that very day, and from the first words

7 o'clock: Wake up.

I felt a wave of relief.

Of course, things didn't fall into place right away. After

7 o'clock: Wake up.

I wrote

7:01:   Feet on floor. Out of bed.
7:02:   To the bathroom. Urinate.
7:03:   Brush teeth.
7:04:   Floss teeth, rinse.
7:05:   Walk leisurely from bathroom to
         kitchen.
7:06:   Pause to remember a voice.
7:07:   Emotional interlude: longing.
7:08:   Think about breakfast on way to
         kitchen.
7:09:   Reject preceding thought.
         Leave kitchen.

And so on . . .

There was more solace in the elaboration of a timetable than there was in its execution. I fastidiously set down the minutes in a day, all of them. There were 1,440 entries on 43 pages, but I'd forgotten to leave time to read them.

You understand, I knew how strange it was to wander about the house, pacing myself, reading from my pages, and once the comfort of precision faded, I was not confident of my state of mind.

And yet, I'd done some things right. The minutes of sleep were easily accomplished, and I had wisely left myself "emotional interludes," though I'd forgotten how unpredictable they are. (I remember staring at a cup for three hours one day, won-

22

dering why it was yellow. It's difficult to schedule an episode like that.)

The trick, which I have almost mastered, is latitude.

Looking over the pages I've written so far, I have the distinct feeling my childhood was unpleasant.

It wasn't, not entirely.

My grandmother was a frightening woman, but even she occasionally lost herself in good humor. There was pumpkin pie for Halloween, Christmas cake for Christmas, plum pudding and ice cream whenever the mood struck her.

Petrolia was unexciting, but it was also a stillness: an impossibly delicate tree frog in the palm of my hand, milkweeds and thistles, acres and acres of green and ochre, the dark stubble that sticks up from under snow-flattened fields . . .

I might even have said my early childhood was good, if I hadn't decided to write it, to write about the others who populated it.

There's nothing to be done, though. The way to Katarina and Henry is through me.

Our neighbors to the east, the Schwartzes, were a little ominous.

They moved into their ivy-covered house when I was six.

I'd been admiring centipedes when I heard the sound of a hard rubber ball, *tock*ing, and then the voice of a girl, singing.

I looked through the hedge and saw Irene Schwartz lazily dropping a rubber ball on a wobbly pane of slate.

— What're you doing? I asked.

— Nothing, she answered.

— You live here?

— Yes, she said

and went back to the rubber ball and slate. Not a promising beginning.

— You're not supposed to play in the hedge, she said. It could wither.

— It won't wither.

— My mother said it will.

I withdrew from the hedge in disgust. That was the problem with young girls, there was more amusement in counting centipedes.

After a while, Irene herself poked through the hedge.

— Boy from next door? she called.

— What?

— We have juice and cookies at my house.

I'd heard stories about Mrs. Schwartz before I met her or Irene. First, there was no man in the house. Then, they kept a candle in their back window, an inexplicable candle, lit at night. Why?

My grandmother disliked them entirely, and the Goodman girls thought Mrs. Schwartz must be a witch, a real witch with children trapped in the basement, and jars of human fingers.

So, I was wary when we met.

Irene was almost as tall as I. Her hair was short and wavy, her eyes light blue, and her ears stuck out.

We entered their kitchen through the back door. I sat at the table, beside a window. The window was open, but the place smelled of apples, and there was something simmering on the stove.

— Can we have some cookies, please? Irene shouted.

And Mrs. Schwartz came in. She said

— Irene, who's your friend?

— The boy from next door.

— And does the boy next door have a name?

— I don't know.

I struggled with the silence before answering.

— Thomas, I said.

— Thomas . . . You're Katarina's son, aren't you?

— I guess so.

— How nice to meet you. We'll have to have cookies and lemonade to celebrate.

Nothing in Mrs. Schwartz's demeanor either confirmed or controverted her being a witch. She was kind and attentive, but what better tack to choose with children you wanted to eat?

Her appearance was suggestive of neither good nor evil. She was slender and redheaded. Her shoulders sloped slightly. Her nose was narrow, but not overlong, and her eyes were blue.

Once the lemonade was finished, she shook my hand, firmly, and invited me back.

My second impression of Mrs. Schwartz was more striking.

On a gloomy day, sunless, the air smelling of rain and tar, Irene and I were outside, jumping to

> *Peas porridge hot,*
> *Peas porridge cold,*
> *Peas porridge in the pot,*
> *Nine days old.*
> *How many bowlsful do you want?*

We were neither of us very good. I spent most of the time halfheartedly watching Irene, the way her dress billowed. And when the rain came, we ran inside, where her mother was frantically closing windows and turning off the lights.

While Irene and I dried our heads, Mrs. Schwartz put candles on the window sills.

— Lightning, she said.

It was dark as night outside. We sat in the living room, trying to ignore the lightning, listening to the thunder. I could smell my wet clothes, the candles, the house itself.

Mrs. Schwartz, frightened by the weather, talked on and on: rain is good for the garden, thunder is the voice of God, we are all water . . .

She also told two stories, one about a certain Mr. Smith, the other about a certain Mr. Jones.[4]

---

[4] There was once a man named Smith. Every morning at seven, he would drive to work in Sarnia, and every evening he would return. His life was dull. It was a meek resistance to death until, one night, as he was driving home, his car broke down. It was winter, and he was miles from home. There was a farmhouse half a mile from where he'd stopped, and he trudged through deep snow to get to it. He knocked at the door, and after a very long time an old man answered. The man's face was round and white as a drum.

— What is it this time? he asked, holding the door open just enough to let his face out.

When Mr. Smith explained his predicament, the old man said

— You know damn well I don't have a phone!

and shut the door.

It was a bitterly cold night. The moon was white. Mr. Smith's breath was thick as smoke. He knocked again.

— Well? the old man answered.

— Could I come in for a few minutes, to warm up?

The old man spat on him and closed the door.

Mr. Smith walked back to his car, his hands in his pockets, his feet cold, his face burning. He had just decided to trudge back home when

To this day, I remember the sound of her voice, the way she held her cigarettes, the flickering candlelight.

There was something reassuring in her fear of lightning.

Were it not for Lillian Schwartz, the world of my childhood might have been one-dimensional in time. I knew nothing of my grandmother, save what I observed, and nothing at all about my mother.

---

he saw a small boy standing by the side of the road. The boy was about five years old, his hair white with snow, and he was dressed in summer clothes. He stood near Mr. Smith's car, shivering.

— Please, take me with you, the boy said.

It was a pathetic sight. Mr. Smith took off his coat, wrapped it around the boy, and together they went back to the farmhouse. This time Mr. Smith knocked with determination. The old man answered, slowly, as before, but when he saw the child he said

— Get away!

and tried to close the door. Mr. Smith grabbed the old man's nose and squeezed for all he was worth. The old man pleaded

— But I don't want to go!

He moved backward to free himself, and Mr. Smith and the boy went in.

The next thing happened very quickly. Mr. Smith let go of the old man's nose. The old man fell. The boy turned into a large black dog. The dog pounced on the old man and bit his throat. The old man didn't even have time to scream. His neck snapped, and he died.

You can imagine the effect all of this had on Mr. Smith. He was paralyzed with fear. He shivered as the dog licked its maw and cleaned the blood from its coat.

— I'll be with you in a minute, the dog said.

— Take your time, said Mr. Smith.

Finally, the dog turned to Mr. Smith and said

It's through Lillian Schwartz that I learned the small things I know about Edna and Katarina MacMillan, the details that give their deaths, years apart though they were, even deeper resonance in my imagination.

And yet, in remembering her, I most vividly remember things that Lillian Schwartz remembered. She herself doesn't always figure in the memories I have of her. This makes proper order a little difficult. I feel I should proceed as follows:

But I may be slipping into poetry.

1 Edna MacMillan

Apparently, my grandmother wasn't always slovenly. In Lillian's memory, she was conscientious and efficient.

— Didn't you know you were his death?

— No, said Mr. Smith.

— You know, said the dog thoughtfully, there are no bounds to human ignorance . . .

And it moved like a shadow out of the farmhouse and into the night.

From that moment, Mr. Smith was a changed man.

He avoided farmhouses, and he rarely went out in winter.

Her life, but for the years in Trinidad, was lived in Petrolia, and Petrolia crushed everything else from her so thoroughly that I could not have guessed her origins were anything but Canadian.[5]

She began teaching in her twenties and infected countless children with the verse of Archibald Lampman. She retired at sixty-five, just in time to take care of her grandson, Thomas MacMillan, myself.

For years, her home was a haven to the Dickens Society of Lambton County. That is, she was host to a group of women from Petrolia, Oil City, and Oil Springs who met on Grove Street to eat plum pudding, whatever the season, and discuss the novels of Charles Dickens.

The novels, scrupulously chosen by my grandmother, were parsed to within an inch of their lives and made to yield the secrets of character.

It was at the center of the Dickens Society that she flourished.

That's not to say my grandmother was blameless in either of the misfortunes that soured her life: the dissolution of the Dickens Society; the death of her husband. Her temper was always erratic. She could be mean-spirited and unyielding, and she was prone to bouts of "sensitivity" that made the company of others intolerable.

In her old age, these aspects of her personality grew more pronounced, but they didn't come out of the blue.

---

[5] It's true that the flag of Trinidad is the same red, white, and black as my grandmother's dresses, but that was a coincidence, I think. The island gained its independence in 1962, long after she'd left it, long after it had ceased to matter to her.

1.1 End of the Dickens Society of Lambton County

As far as reading groups go, the Dickens Society seems to have been successful. It existed from 1946 to 1949, turbulent years for the world, difficult years for Petrolia.

The women met on the first Tuesday of every month, in the evening.

— Your grandmother's house always smelled of plum pudding and rose water . . .

Lillian Schwartz's mother, Edwina Martin, "Eedy" to my grandmother's "Eddy," was a faithful participant and, in consequence, so was Lillian. Her father was not expected to "work all day *and* mind the child at night."

It was on these evenings, under the aegis of the Dickens Society, that Katarina and Lillian became friends. They were both eight years of age when the group began. They had the run of the house, as long as they kept out from under my grandfather's feet.

Though the women were, individually, conservative, the reading group itself was lively. They had opinions and ideas that they put boldly forth, goaded by my grandmother's dandelion brandy. They were even, at times, almost raucous in their sympathies and loathings for Abel Magwitch, say, or Bill Sykes.

Then my grandfather would come in to quiet them.

— Ladies, please!

And their voices would subside, and then rise again until it was nine o'clock, time to go home.

Though Lillian was too young to appreciate its causes, the Society's passions left an impression.

Aside from my grandmother and Lillian's mother, there were two women from Oil City (one of whom smelled of rose water) and two sisters: Mrs. Ellen Benjamin (Oil Springs) and Mrs. Margaret Grossman (Petrolia).

Mrs. Ellen, who was wealthy, read the novels and occasionally gave an opinion, but it seems she was there to humor her sister, whom she treated with scorn.

— How can you be so stupid? she'd hiss

or

— That's the silliest thing you've said yet.

Her words had a withering effect on her sister. A timid woman to begin with, Mrs. Margaret rarely volunteered an idea that was not an echo of her sister's. Even at that, she stroked her amethyst brooch before speaking and the fingers on her right hand were almost always bandaged.

Most of the women disliked Mrs. Ellen's high-handedness. They resented her jabs at her sister's intelligence. None of the others had wealthy husbands or swank pearls, and they took Mrs. Ellen's condescension personally.

— She doesn't think her own farts stink

is how Lillian's mother expressed it.

My grandmother, on the other hand, unequivocally took Mrs. Ellen's side. She couldn't stand spinelessness. She bullied Mrs. Margaret almost as often as Mrs. Ellen did, dismissing her opinions even when she might have agreed with them.

In the winter of 1948, at what was to be the Society's last full meeting, the novel in question was that most dangerous of books: *Our Mutual Friend*.

Lillian and Katarina were bored. They'd spent most of the evening trying to sip from the tumblers of brandy while the Society argued.

And there seems to have been a great deal to argue about.

Mr. Wrayburn was too much this or too that. He was wealthy, but his character was clouded. He was anti-Semitic, but he was noble. He was noble, but indolent. He was indolent, but charming. And, though the ending was happy, there was much doubt as to his value as a husband.

Mrs. Ellen, who took affront at this insult to a wealthy man, began to berate the poor. The poor who—like a certain *Mr.* Grossman, the janitor at St. Philip's—weren't any fitter for marriage, with their mothballs, penny candles, and kerosene lamps.

— But, said Mrs. Margaret, a man isn't a change purse.

— What do you know about change purses? her sister answered. Two sticks to rub together you haven't got.

Mrs. Margaret meekly repeated her point as her sister and my grandmother mounted their assault.

— You're taking this personally, you silly woman.

And the young girls watched in amazement as the Society lost itself in personal invective.

— To hell with money!

— To hell with Oil City!

After which, there was no turning back. Such foul language. Even in jest, it was an insult to my grandmother's home.

The other women were giddy with daring. They battered Mrs. Ellen so thoroughly that she sat as though starched, facing them only with the scorn of the outnumbered.

During all this, Mrs. Margaret sat patiently, mindless of the catastrophe, repeating her one simple note

— A man isn't a purse . . .

as if it were still a question of Dickens and change purses.

— Be quiet, my grandmother said

her voice almost lost amid the voices around her, no one quite sure whom it was she wanted quiet.

Then, as Mrs. Margaret was about to speak, my grandmother stood up and slapped the woman's face.

The others sat stunned while Mrs. Margaret repeated her

— But . . . but . . . but . . .

Mrs. Ellen rose and put on her coat.

— You see? she said to Mrs. Margaret.

She helped her sister up from the chair, on with her coat, and, without another word, they walked out of the house.

The remaining members of the Dickens Society were, understandably, nervous in my grandmother's company from then on.

They gathered on a few more occasions, but without enthusiasm, and they made no effort to replace the two sisters.

Three years after it began, the Society died a quiet but undignified death.

For years afterward, stories of my grandmother's disgrace were widespread. She had spit at Mrs. Ellen; she had damaged Mrs. Ellen's automobile; she had pinched Mrs. Margaret; she had bitten Mrs. Margaret; she had thrown dishes; she had thrown food. Was she really fit to teach young children? She wasn't "all there," now, was she?

The Dickens Society of Lambton County expired in the early months of 1949, and its death must have been a humiliating thing for my grandmother.

It was a humiliating thing for me as well.

I finally understood why some of the adults treated me with exaggerated sympathy or exaggerated scorn, why the janitor at St. Philip's could not stand the sight of me.

1.2 The Death of Her Husband

My grandfather, for whom I was named, is something of an enigma. I never heard the sound of his voice. I never felt his touch and, until my grandmother's death, I had no idea what he looked like.

The only marks of his passage were the signatures he left in his books.

It was like following a stranger down the aisles of a library, stopping to look at the books he's touched (Lucretius, Liddell's *Lexicon*, a complete Shakespeare, a book on gardening), speaking to those with whom he has spoken (my mother, my grandmother, Mrs. Schwartz).

— What did he say? What was he like?

— I can't remember . . .

— I don't remember . . .

— He was kind . . .

What can you know of someone like that? He seems to have been a man of wide, if musty, learning. The signature in his books is always faint, as if in apology. The dandelion wine and the dandelion brandy were *his* idea, though they were more pernicious in my grandmother's life than they were in his.

(I do feel something of his presence in myself, but it's unclassifiable, a subtraction of other presences.)

For me, the most remarkable thing about him is that, for almost thirty years, from 1922 until his death in 1950, he lived with my grandmother, not an uncomplicated woman.

Of course, she loved him.

The particulars of my grandfather's death, of which there appear to have been witnesses, are as follows:

1. It was a sunny day. (Sunlight circa 1950.)
2. My grandparents were at a corner on Petrolia Street.
3. My grandparents were speaking of something.
4. My grandfather stepped off the curb.
5. He was struck by a car.

It would be tidy to leave it at that: a chain of events with drama, atmosphere, tension, and surprise. But the things that make this death a wound are in the possible circumstances around the moment, in the details of the details:

It was a sunny day. An odd fact, provided by Mrs. Schwartz. I take it to mean that my grandfather's vision was not impaired by natural phenomena. He might have seen the car coming, if only he'd looked up, or looked in the right direction. Something, or someone, prevented his looking, or distracted him from it altogether. There was no real darkness, but the door is open for another kind of dark.

My grandparents were at a corner on Petrolia Street. Being from Petrolia, there's nothing unusual about that. They were at a place they knew intimately, crossing from here to there on a street they must have crossed thousands of times, each crossing but this one unfateful. There was nothing ominous about where they stood, but how many times thereafter must my grandmother have asked herself: Why here? What if we'd crossed farther on?

My grandparents were speaking of something. Again, what could be more innocent? They would have exchanged a world's worth of words in their life together. But what if she were scolding him? What if it was *she* who drew his attention from the street? Well, then, there's the darkness: cloud cover provided by my grandmother herself.

My grandfather
stepped off the
curb.

In one version of the world, this is the fateful instant in three lives: my grandmother's, my mother's, and mine. As my grandfather steps down and turns his head toward his wife to say "What?" or "Really, Edna, I . . ." three small miseries take shape: my grandmother's years of loneliness and guilt, my mother's intense rebellion, and my own childhood. Our lives break off from that moment, as neatly as if he were stepping down on a pane of glass. And then . . .

He was struck by   My grandfather died.
a car.

Like all good stories, it sounds so plausible. How wonderful to imagine that, but for a misstep, our lives might have taken a happier course, that my grandmother loved me, but she was distracted by stronger emotions.

> Thomas: *(wistfully)* Gosh! If only the old man had
> looked where he was going . . .

The thing is, it won't wash, even for me who wishes it.

Edna MacMillan must certainly have gone through hell watching the man she loved die on the street. (She had married late, at thirty, old enough to know why she wanted him, and, at fifty-eight, she was old enough to know what she was losing.) It may even have driven her to more excessive drink or begun a rift between her and her daughter.

But all this is just modest guessing, and the details are so clearly speculative they make a paltry, therapeutic fiction.

Who's to say our lives would have been happier with my

grandfather alive? How can I know what my grandmother felt (guilt? relief? nothing at all?)? She never spoke to me of her Thomas's death.

Though I feel this death's importance for our lives, the only things I know about it are: sun, street, talk, step, car, death.

2 Katarina MacMillan

In some versions of her father's death, Katarina insisted it was her mother who pushed him under the car.

In others, she was there, twelve years old, a horrified witness.

In still others, she was in school, called from the classroom by Mr. Lapierre, his hand on her shoulder as he bent down to whisper, so softly she didn't know who died.

My mother wasn't a liar, you understand. That would have been too easy. Rather, over the years, she told innumerable versions of the incidents that upset her.

I take the number of renditions, and their variety, as proof her father's death was especially traumatic. Her imagination wouldn't let it be.

My mother's life was so full of commotion, I'm grateful she found the calm to parturate. Still, the decision to have me at all is typically contrary. It shows her romantic streak, her intense but intermittent regard for Love, Family, and Home.

What am I saying? I'm less than grateful where my birth is concerned, but I can imagine my mother's willful joy at the thought of me.

All the more surprising, then, that the young girl Lillian Schwartz remembered is someone else entirely, a good friend, constant and fearless.

I saw her in that light first.

———

Whenever I asked if my mother's Petrolia was like the one I inhabited, Mrs. Schwartz's response was

— Nothing changes.

If I pressed her about this or that, a new building, say, or a fancy house, she would say

— Plus ça change . . .

an idea I wouldn't understand for decades, if I understand it at all.

I wanted to visit the places my mother visited, to discover whatever there might be of Katarina in them, instinctively feeling that Petrolia, the town itself, its trees and bridges, fields and houses, was our point of contact. So, it was a disappointment to learn that Lillian Schwartz didn't know as much about my mother's childhood as I'd hoped.

Still, they were in the same class at St. Philip's, Lillian and Katarina, with girls named Eunice and boys named Michael.

— Five Michaels in grade three alone.

Their teachers, including my grandmother, were strict and Catholic.

They attended St. Philip's Church, towed by their mothers.

(My grandmother Catholic? That was a revelation.)

Their homes were certainly different.

Lillian was the youngest of four children, and though the sibling nearest her in age was seven years older, there was company. There were others on whom her mother could dote; four to take the weight of their parents' care.

Mr. Martin, fourteen years a postman at Lillian's birth, a postman thirty-six years when he died, was a loving man. He was short and portly, and his hair was inevitably brush cut. He had a voice from God, though, a beautiful tenor with which he sang the children to sleep. It was one of Mrs. Schwartz's regrets that, at the proud age of ten, she made him stop because she was too old for lullabies.

Mrs. Martin, whose relationship with my grandmother did not survive the death of the Dickens Society, was more circumspect with Katarina. She understood how it might be difficult to live with Edna MacMillan. She was even sympathetic, but she saw something of Edna in Katarina and was put off.

— Just you wait, she said, till Katarina's tired of playing goody-goody.

Mrs. Martin was wary of a certain tendency in Negroes, a tendency that was sure to show itself, however good Katarina might appear on the surface. Katarina was even darker than Edna, and look at Edna . . . she had hoodwinked people into treating her white, and no good came of that, just you ask poor Mrs. Margaret, who, by the by, didn't deserve to be slapped and kicked.

— Once bitten, twice shy.

2.1 She Is Good

My mother first revealed her generosity at the age of eleven, when both girls had a crush on Michael Stone.

Michael lived two streets west of Grove. He also attended St. Philip's. He was not physically remarkable or even particularly cute, but he was gentler than the other boys in grade seven.

He may not even have been so gentle. It's just that his glasses, their frames, suggested a kind of gentleness, and he was painfully self-conscious, as you might expect from a boy who couldn't see without his glasses.

They suspected him of "having a past," an extraordinary suspicion to have of an eleven-year-old. His lack of interest in girls they took for proof of a tragic side.

The girls discovered their shared interest in Michael as they went over the list of their classmates, deciding whom they liked and whom they didn't.

It was a ritual they performed weekly, sometimes daily.

— Cindy?

— She's okay.

— Pauline?

— I like her.

— Me too.

— Donna?

— I like her.

— Did you see how she . . . ?

And when it came to the third or fourth Michael, the one who sat beside the window, Katarina said

— He's a dream.

Lillian said

— He's such a dream.

They spent hours deciding who liked him most. Did Kata like him more than Terry Johnson? A little. Did Lillian like him more than Frank Moore? A little.

— Would you . . .   (kiss)

— Would you?

— And would you . . .   (kiss in public)

— No! Would you?

— Maybe . . . circumstances permitting . . .

After intense consideration, Kata decided it was Lillian who really cared for Michael.

Not only did she withdraw from the race for his affection, but she managed to persuade Lillian that the thing she and Michael needed was "time alone." She was so persuasive that Lillian, who hadn't realized how deep her feelings were, began to anticipate her moments with him.

The tricky part was Michael himself.

They inflicted their attention on him, but he withstood the assault, mildly answering the most coquettish questions.

— Do you like Lillian's dress?

— Are your mother's eyes as green as yours?

He never refused to walk home with them, but he rarely said anything. He didn't exactly brood, but it was like brooding.

He seemed to have no passions at all, nothing to talk about, though, on occasion, he was susceptible to boats. That is, he sometimes ventured an opinion on the subject of shipbuilding or ocean sailing. You couldn't have called it a passion, really. He never went beyond a stifled remark on the *Bluenose* or the *Queen Elizabeth*, but that was enough for Kata.

With what was, even for an eleven-year-old, idiosyncratic thinking, she persuaded Lillian to wear blue as often as she could: blue shoes, blue barrettes, blue socks.

Then she herself asked Lillian's father how it was possible to build ships in bottles. She spoke as if a ship in a bottle were the thing she wanted most in the world, though she doubted it could be done by any but an expert.

This was the part I found most admirable. It wasn't that Mr. Martin was a difficult adult to play. He would have done anything to please the children. But the variables . . . First, would Mr. Martin fall for her approach? (He did.) Second, could he actually build a ship in a bottle? (He could.) Third, how long would it take? (A month.) Fourth, was the bottled replica of a galleon the thing to lure Michael from his shell? (Well . . .)

When the blue of Lillian's clothes had had time to work its spell, and when Mr. Martin had completed his minuscule but slightly ragged galleon, which rattled in its dark-green bottle, Katarina casually mentioned the ship as the three of them were walking home.

Wouldn't Michael like to see it up close?

— Sure, he answered.

This story fascinated me for years. Not only was it about my mother, but in my mother's tactics I saw a love of detail that I shared, though it would never have occurred to me to bring such precision to bear on personal matters.

Given: Michael Stone, hereafter (Mst)
            Lillian Martin, hereafter (Lm)
Variables: Mr. Martin (MrM), Ships (S), Blue (B)
Environment: Martins' Home (MH)

Problem: *Using the elements given, and the*
            variables at one's disposal, how is it
            possible to combine (Mst) and (Lm)
            without adversely affecting the given
            environment (MH)?

Even now, knowing my mother failed math and geography, that she would not have seen things in quite this way, I am filled with admiration.

There is, in any intense calculation, such a longing for tranquillity that I almost pity her.

And the result of her planning *was* "(Mst) + (Lm)."

Michael Stone expectantly entered the Martins' home looking for a ship. Neither of Lillian's parents was there at the time, and the bottled galleon, which was usually on the mantelpiece, just happened to be in Lillian's room.

And when Katarina left the two of them together, on the pretext that she wanted a peanut butter sandwich but actually to watch out for Mr. or Mrs. Martin, Lillian and Michael did, eventually, kiss.

Mrs. Schwartz:	First in a long line of disappointments.
Thomas:	But why?
Mrs. Schwartz:	(*mysterious smile*) You'll see.

Though the kiss was disappointing for Lillian, it was a revelation to Michael.

From the moment their lips touched, he was lost. He began to sweat, his glasses slipped, his face reddened, and, not knowing where else to put them, he put his hands on top of his head.

All of which only deepened Lillian's disappointment. And in that disappointment, there was an inkling of their misjudgment. She and Katarina had assumed Michael was gentle but dark, that his wordlessness was world-weary like the wordless men they knew from books. Now she suspected he would have come to the Martins' without Katarina's elaborate prompting.

It's not that Lillian knew Michael's was less than a real kiss. It was her first. But the discovery that he was run-of-the-mill—not cute, not funny, not brooding—*that* was hard to bear.

After that, kissing Michael was like kissing a fish.

The thing is, Kata had done so much on Lillian's behalf, and the intensity of Michael's feelings wasn't unflattering. It was a little intoxicating even. So, when their kiss finally ended and Michael was pushed from her room and persuaded to go home and Kata said

— Tell me, tell me . . .

Lillian gave a swooning account of the interlude.

— Oh, it was so . . . he's so . . .

— I just knew it!

Over the next ten months, or until the Stones left for Smiths

Falls, Lillian allowed Michael to press his lips against hers, from time to time, to Katarina's great satisfaction.

2.2 She Is Fearless

I wrote earlier that, in setting my life down, I thought I might be slipping into poetry.

You would think, given my long history with the art, that I'd have made my peace with poetry. It saved me from a thrashing. My grandmother had me memorize it, a discipline she'd also imposed on Katarina. So, it is a grievance my mother and I shared.

It is also one of the things Henry loved most in this world.

It pains me to read it, though. It's an abyss.

When I first saw you, for instance, I was blissfully reading the *Notebooks of Samuel Butler*. You were reading the poetry of Osip Mandelshtam. I saw the book before I saw you. You held the gray covers apart, the little finger on your right hand curled up like a snail. (I adore your hands.)

As soon as you left, I pulled the Mandelshtam across the table, curious:

> *There is no need for speech*
> *And nothing to teach;*
> *How sad, yet beautiful*
> *Is the dark brutal soul.*

I read those lines over and over, trying to imagine the two of us, heads touching, one of us speaking, or speaking them together. And then I suddenly felt lost, lost as in adrift.

What in God's name takes you from speech to teach, from sadness to beauty, from beauty to the soul?

What is a "dark brutal soul" anyway?

I understood the words, but I felt as much distress as understanding. I wondered where my understanding came from. Is it Mandelshtam who gives it sense? Do the words themselves make sense? Or is it, finally, one's own self that understands in its own way?

You could scratch your head over those questions for years, and the second stanza only made things worse:

> *It has nothing it wants to teach*
> *And lacks even the power of speech,*
> *But like a young dolphin swims*
> *Where the world's gray deeps are dim.*

End of poem.

Now, how in the world did that young dolphin get in there? How did we go from soul to dolphin? The more I forced myself to bring "soul" and "dolphin" together, the less contact I felt with the outside world.

I learned about my self, perhaps; that I could bring them together, that for an instant, there, my soul did swim in the dark.

A thoroughly unpleasant experience.

Poetry's all well and good if you need reasons to go inside, but, as you know, I've always needed reasons to go out. (How often you've tried to turn my attention to the world, and how often I've resisted. Until I met you, the *Ottawa Citizen* was as much of the world as I could take.)

I'm not alone, either. My grandmother should never have read a line. Lampman was her abyss of choice, when she was lucid enough to choose—not much difference between wine and poetry, now that I think of it, and she'd have been better off without either of them.

Perhaps I missed something.

Perhaps, to you, the poem is not abstract, but it's the inebriating chaos that makes me nervous.

After her father's death, Katarina changed.

He died when she was twelve, and one might have expected a little introspection and gloom, but it was just the opposite. While turning away from the people around her, she became more outward, more expressive, less demure.

This was difficult for me to understand, until I met my mother.

> Katarina: (*softly, because she rarely raised her voice*)
> You've got hard heels. Let me see your feet.
> Hold still . . .
> Thomas: You're hurting me.
> Katarina: That doesn't hurt. Everyone knows children
> and animals don't feel pain. Your spinal
> columns aren't developed.

That was typical of my mother. She was cutting the calluses from my heels with a straight razor. It *did* hurt and I resented her lack of sympathy, but my heels had cracked and bled. What could she do?

And, oddly enough, I was so intrigued by the idea that my spinal column was undeveloped, I sat still.

> Katarina: There. Now put your socks on.

What I mean is, as grief for her father was expressed in an unusual way, so too was her affection for me.

And I know that surface rarely mirrors depth, but with my mother it was more so.

At sixteen, without arguing, without even agreeing to go their own ways, Lillian and Katarina went their own ways; this though Katarina had begun to spend more time with the Martins and less with her mother.

She and Edna had gone from dutiful tolerance to open discord.

It would have been cruel for my mother to abandon her own home entirely. Everyone in town knew both Katarina *and* her mother. Where could she have gone without further damaging Edna MacMillan's reputation? It had been only five years since my grandmother's now legendary assault on Mrs. Grossman. Katarina cared enough to spare her further shame.

So, though she kept her own hours, she slept at her mother's or, as often as was acceptable, at the Martins'.

Time with the Martins was not a release from the predicaments of home.

Mrs. Martin never really accepted Katarina. She was even less sympathetic now that Katarina showed clear signs of being Black: keeping her own hours, neglecting her schoolwork, spending too much time with the Thériauxes and Maisonneuves, "the poorest families in town."

> Lillian: They weren't poor, they were French. Not even.
> The kids couldn't speak a word of it, but their
> parents had French accents. My mother never
> trusted them. That's just how she was, Thomas.
> My own *father* was French Canadian.

Mrs. Martin worried about the influence Katarina might have on her daughter. That was the problem. Though she never said anything directly, and never once turned her out, she did the little things that one can do to drive a point. She asked leading questions.

— How's your mother, Kata? Do you see much of her?

or

— You're so mature for your age. Are you really thinking of leaving home? You know, we have so little room here.

She conspicuously neglected to serve Katarina when the family was at table.

— Oh, I didn't realize you were staying for supper. I'm sorry, Kata.

She constantly grumbled, to no one in particular, about the laundry that had to be done.

You would have to have been a blockhead to misunderstand.

Katarina was not.

The girls' last friendly moment came when they were sixteen.

It was July or it was August, a warm night. The two of them were reading together.

They read until it was late and the house was quiet.

Mr. and Mrs. Martin were asleep, and Lillian herself was already in pajamas when Kata said

— Why don't we go out?

That was something they hadn't done forever, go out and look at the stars. And thinking they were going down to the backyard and the wooden lawn chairs her father had just finished, Lillian put on a dirty dress, an old shirt, and running shoes.

It was just as well she put on the shoes, because that night "out" was a long walk through the sleeping town: moonlit, the houses two-dimensional against the sky.

It was the first time Lillian saw the town as almost exotic, though she knew all of the houses by heart and most of the people who lived in them.

They walked a mile from town in the near quiet, giggling past the MacPhersons' orchard, their crab apples.

— The most vicious dogs to guard the least tempting fruit.

And then they were at the gravel pit, an excavation filled with rainwater, another pool to drown the region's youth, there being no shore, no gradual decline, only the pool itself, said to be nine feet deep or twenty feet deep or deep as the ocean, unsounded.

It wasn't Lillian's idea to swim. She'd known two of the children who'd drowned there. Katarina undressed and dove into the water.

— Come in, she said. It's warm.

It would have been faithless to stand beside the quarry and watch, so Lillian too undressed. The shore, such as it was, was rock-strewn. She tiptoed to the water and slid in. The water was warm. The air smelled of weeds. The moon was bright.

It was thrilling, and it wasn't only the warmth, the moon, and the stars that made her ecstatic. It was swimming with Kata, their small bodies engulfed in . . .

Thomas: You were naked?
Mrs. Schwartz: Of course. Your mother was a beautiful young woman. Much more attractive than me.

They swam until they were exhausted, then dragged themselves from the water and put on their clothes.

Arm in arm, for warmth, they walked back, past the same fields and farmhouses, past the barbershop and the bakery, along the tarred streets, along which, in their dark houses, there lived the Lafleurs, the MacDonalds, the Del Monicos, the Smiths, the Smyths, the Howards, the Wilsons . . .

She was certain no one saw them, though she was so elated she wouldn't have minded if they had.

The two of them swimming: a moment of pure, innocent pleasure.

Lillian Schwartz never learned how her parents discovered she'd been to the quarry, but they saw the swim in a different light.

For Mrs. Martin, it was as if her daughter were on the road to ruin. It was only the lowest who went to the quarry, and this, this skinny-dipping with Kata and God knows who else, it was unspeakable.

The door to their house was closed to Katarina MacMillan.

Mr. Martin, though he was genuinely fond of Katarina, nodded sadly at the edict. It wouldn't do to roughhouse at the quarry.

— But we were only swimming.

— Only swimming? said Mrs. Martin. Thank heavens and what's next? Only drinking? Only kissing? Only . . .

And that was the last they spoke of Katarina.

At the news of her ostracism, my mother turned to Lillian and said

— So what?

her last words to any of the Martins.

The end of their friendship broke Lillian's heart.

She felt the injustice of her parents' behavior, it's true, but Katarina's refusal to speak to her was as painful as if the two had been in love. Besides, it left a question unanswered. Who told on them?

I have considered the question myself.

If the story is true and *if* no one saw them as they walked through town and *if* Lillian never spoke of their swim to anyone but Katarina, then the death of their friendship was almost certainly Katarina's doing.

Mrs. Schwartz was too kind to say so, but I know she blamed my mother.

For my part, I do feel my mother's presence in all this, but I don't understand whose needs were served.

If she'd meant to sever her ties to the Martins, why bother to go swimming at all? If she'd wanted to blacken Lillian's reputation, why lead her to the quarry? A lie would have done as well.

There are too many missing pieces. I can't follow the logic.

3 Mrs. Schwartz and the Candle at Night

I find it odd that I have so few memories of Lillian Schwartz herself.

She was a generous woman, and fascinating. From the beginning, I was enthralled by her stories of Katarina. I first heard them when I was six or seven, and in them, through her, I lived in friendship with my mother.

I remember the color of Lillian Schwartz's eyes, the color of her hair . . . but, if it comes to that, I remember her house, its rooms, in more vivid detail.

Most vividly, I remember the rumors that preceded her.

It was the Goodman girls who taught me the significance of living beside a witch. If Mrs. Schwartz was a witch, and most of the children in the neighborhood agreed she was, then I should look out for the following:

i. *Missing Children, Their Cries*

Because witches ate children, there were bound to be disappearances. Should I ever have the courage to investigate, I would almost certainly find them in the Schwartzes' basement. And, if I ever managed to stay up late, when the town was quiet, I would almost certainly hear their sniveling, close as our house was to theirs.

ii. *Odors*

Well, it would be difficult to hide the smell of missing children, alive or dead. And, because witches were unable to eat a whole child at one go, there were certain to be mason jars everywhere: jars of fingers, toes, and things. The bigger pieces, hands and feet for instance, would be in Tupperware. Legs and arms would have to be kept in a refrigerator, though that wouldn't keep them from stinking. So, it followed that she would use exotic perfumes and cans of air freshener, anything to disguise the pickling.

iii. *Cats*

An essential companion, usually black, though a black dog would do.

iv. *Miscellaneous*

The following might be proof, but you couldn't count on them, witches having changed with the times: long noses, big chins, black hats, black clothes, black books, brooms, cauldrons, toadstools, goats, frenzied dancing around an open fire . . .

It's difficult to imagine how Mrs. Schwartz acquired her reputation among the children on Grove.

She was a hard-oiler, forever belonging because she was born in Petrolia. She'd left town to marry a man from Strathroy, yes, but she hadn't stayed away long. Her family was well known. Her father was fondly remembered for years after his death. Even her daughter, who should have been tainted by association, was more warmly greeted than she was. No one thought Irene evil, just unfortunate.

It's true that, if one looked with an eye to witchery, the signs were almost there. There were no children hidden in her house, but there were mason jars on shelves all over the basement, jars filled with plants and roots that did resemble toes and manikins. The house usually smelled of whatever was cooking, but she herself wore patchouli, a most exotic perfume for the time. (I mean, once she'd named it and encouraged me to breathe the air at her wrist, I never smelled patchouli but in her presence.) She had no conspicuous black books, save for a Bible, but she did have one that included pictures of wolves walking on their hind legs.

For the first months after the Schwartzes moved into the house beside our own, I looked for something to allay my fears. However, fear only briefly troubled my imagination. It didn't survive our first conversations about Katarina.

I mention all this only to explain why it was I lay awake at night, listening for the sound of children sniveling. And it was on one of those nights I acquired my most vivid memory of Mrs. Schwartz herself.

The window in my bedroom looked down on the Schwartzes' yard. I could see the back of their house, most of the backyard and, window open, I could smell their garden: marjoram, dill, sweet cicely, parsley . . .

On this night, I was awake long after my bedtime. The house was quiet and stifling. From my vantage, I could see a candle in the Schwartzes' kitchen window, flickering. It was mesmerizing, if only because I was convinced the lace curtains would catch fire.

I could hear the wind through the trees, a sound I've always found soothing. I might even have fallen asleep at my windowsill, looking up at the stars, listening to the wind, but, in the way that one does on the edge of sleep, I suddenly realized I'd been listening to voices.

I couldn't tell how long they'd been speaking or how long I'd been listening, but there they were. One of the voices was that of Mrs. Schwartz; the other was familiar, but it wasn't until she stepped into the moonlight that I recognized Mrs. Goodman.

That in itself was peculiar. I don't think I'd ever seen the two of them together, didn't realize they were close, but here they were, their voices too low for me to make out anything but the occasional word; the two of them side by side looking down at the garden, shoulders almost touching.

Then there was a loud, dry snap, as of a branch breaking.

As one, the women looked in my direction. They could not have seen me, but in my imagination their faces were contorted in anger. I jumped back from the window and onto my bed, truly frightened.

When my heart stopped racing and I found the courage to tiptoe back to the window, the women were gone.

The wind still sounded and the candle burned.

I don't know why I should remember such a trivial moment, but it was so precise and unusual, it was as if I'd dreamed.

It was as if I'd dreamed it at the time. It seems even more improbable now, though I distinctly remember Lillian's face looking up, and I can almost see the candle flame flicker and rise.

IV

However they were in fact, in my mind the Goodmans are associated with death.

I was at the Goodmans' when my grandmother died, or rather, it's to the Goodmans I went for help, on discovering her cold body.

I was infatuated with Margaret Goodman, but our budding relationship died with Edna and with my mother's return.

My mother's return was itself the death of the Katarina Mac-Millan I'd created from the bits and pieces of Mrs. Schwartz's memory.

And, finally, the Goodmans' house was the last building I allowed myself to see as we left Petrolia. I stared at their white house from the car, hoping for a glimpse of Margaret, and then, seeing her with her sisters on their way to school, I closed my eyes so that hers would be the last image I took with me.

Death all around, then. From first love to my mother's return by way of Edna's exit.

I remember every detail of Margaret Goodman's face. I remember it exactly, I think, though I imagine it hasn't looked as I remember it for thirty years.

Even at the time, Margaret's face wasn't Margaret's face. Quite a revelation for a nine-year-old, the idea that Margaret was only really Margaret from the proper angle, or that she was most Margaret when I wasn't looking at her face. Her voice was constant, as was her smell (orange juice). She had a dependable repertoire of clothes and a particular walk, but her face was unpredictable.

I don't mean that she made faces, or that she had a tick. I thought the kids who could make strange faces amusing, but they were mostly boys: Nick Jacob, Mark Gould, Peter Corrigan . . . Nor do I mean that her features were unnaturally mobile. From whatever angle I looked, there were constants: the color of her irises, the dark of her eyebrows, the length of her lashes. These things (irises, eyebrows, lashes) were common to all of her faces, but when I actually looked at her, it was as if they were perpetually out of context.

I found this traumatic.

By the age of nine, I'd already learned to tell a female from a male grasshopper. I knew males were the ones who stridulated. I also knew where to look for ovipositors, could tell the labrum from the labium, the ocelli from the coxae.

It wasn't only a point of pride with me. It was a practical matter.

First, to my grandmother, knowledge—even obscure knowledge—justified time spent at the public library. I was allowed to stay at the library as long as I wanted, but only if, on my return, I could give proof I hadn't spent my time with "sex trash." So, no matter what I was reading, from *Asterix* to Ian Fleming, I memorized a little something from *Collier's Encyclopedia* before going home. (To this day, I can think of few things as beautiful as Collier's cutaway diagrams of the European cabbage butterfly, *Pieris brassicae*, or the human louse, *Pediculus humanus*.)

Second, learning to distinguish fore from hind legs or tibiae from tarsi brought me closer to some of the insects I adored.

Yet, when I first convinced myself of this peculiarity of Margaret's face, it was as if there were something wrong—with me, not her. Not that faces are comparable to insects, but "distinguishing features" were a passion, and it troubled me that Margaret's face was rarely itself.

I felt no anxiety where other faces were concerned. My grandmother's face, though it was just as changeable, was my grandmother's face, whether she was drunk or sober, sitting or tottering, breathing with difficulty or watching television. It wasn't her face that made me anxious.

This aspect of my feelings for Margaret has had the strongest resonance in time. I mean, I'm convinced that the women to whom I've been attracted have all shared certain facial features: eyes, eyelashes, eyebrows. I can trace the similarities from Margaret (the first) to Judita (the last but one). It's not that they've looked alike, but that their faces are the distant echoes of another.

I assume other men are similar, that the faces of the women to whom they're attracted will, on reflection, be similar to another. I also assume it is their mothers who provide the template for whatever they find attractive in the face of this woman or that.

You'd think, having been abandoned by my mother, that none of the women I've admired would look anything like her. Not at all. I'm genuinely alarmed by the resemblance *all* of the women I've loved have had to my mother, even Margaret.

(Yes, even you.)

The face I saw when I closed my eyes was, of all Margaret's faces, the one closest to Katarina's. I hadn't met my mother at that point, so I could not recognize her face in Margaret's. And yet, somewhere inside of me, I'm sure I did.

Margaret Goodman was exactly my age. From 1957, the year of our birth, to 1967, the year I left Petrolia, we lived next door to each other.

I knew all of the Goodman girls, of course. I turned rope for them. They taught me to skip and to use an Easy Bake oven.

I was secretly attracted to Andrea, but Margaret was my first love. Fate, I suppose, and no less bewildering for all that.

In the summer of '66 Margaret's sister Jane was in love with Darren McGuinness.

— I love Alex MacDonald, but I'm *in love* with Darren was how she put it.

The distinction was too mature for me. I didn't really understand it. Besides, I truly, fervently despised Darren and each and every McGuinness who'd ever drawn breath. They were a little collection of Irish vermin whose chief pleasure was to hold me down so the youngest of them, Barry, who was only seven, could strike me with his fists. When their father died of cancer, I wasn't the least bit sorry.

Still, like news from a foreign country that sets wheels turning in one's own, Jane Goodman's love for Darren McGuinness started her sisters thinking. When, from the height of her fifteen years, Jane spoke to us at all, she spoke of

a) life in high school
b) Darren McGuinness.

I listened to the talk about high school, yearning for my own locker, a gymnasium, beakers for chemicals, and "algebra" (the most beautiful name numbers have ever had, I think; *Al-Jabr*, like sugared pomegranate seeds). The girls were impressed by Darren McGuinness. He was sixteen, shared a broken-down

Impala with his older brothers, played baseball *and* basketball, and "really knew how to treat a lady."

There was more, but Jane invariably added

— You're too immature to understand.

(She was referring to that part of courtship, physical intimacy, I still find enigmatic.)

Even so, before that summer was through, both Andrea and Margaret precipitously acquired boyfriends. Andrea chose Don Smith; Margaret chose me.

Objectively speaking, I was an eccentric choice.

First, being Edna MacMillan's grandson I inherited something of her reputation.

— Stable on the outside, eh. Might lose it any time, though. Mrs. MacMillan did quite a number on Jenny Benjamin's mother . . .

And second, Margaret's father could barely conceal his dislike for me; a dislike that had something to do with my grandmother, something to do with natural antipathy, and, I suspect, something to do with Mrs. Schwartz, with whom I spent time.

Yet, despite unpromising prospects, despite my embarrassment on being told

— Andrea and Don are going steady, eh. Why can't we?

I agreed to be her boyfriend and, in the end, found the role intoxicating.[6]

---

[6] I'm always surprised by the force of instinct. It's like the answer you didn't realize you knew to a question asked while you were thinking of something else. Or perhaps it's like a question whose answer has been on the tip of your tongue for days and then, unexpectedly, while you're sleeping, the answer comes to you with such force it wakes you up. Or perhaps it's not like a question at all. Perhaps it's closer to an excruciating itch on an unreachable part of the body, an indescribable need that has gone on for so long it has become a dimension of one's existence. No, actually, perhaps it is like a question after all.

At nine years of age, we were neither of us sure how best to go about steadily. So, with remarkable disinterest, we decided what we would and wouldn't do.

— Hold hands?

— I guess so.

— Should we . . .

— Do you want to?

— I don't think so.

— Ohh . . . okay.

Painlessly, considerate with a consideration I have rarely recovered or received, we

a) kissed once, to see what it was like (uninteresting but not unlikable)

b) held hands (warm, but awkward; not altogether unlikable)

c) shared drinks (rarely, and only if there were straws)

d) walked home together from school (consistently)

e) watched television after school (distressing, because Darren "Hey, I smell nigger" McGuinness was often there with Jane, and Mr. Goodman himself came home at 5:30)

f) played in the Goodmans' backyard (skipping, mostly, along with a handful of girls).

After an autumn of constant company, of having somewhere to go without having to go, after innumerable excursions for Popsicles, ice cream, and licorice, I began to think it wasn't so bad. I wasn't tired of Margaret's company, and I even began to see in her the virtues that make for physical attraction.

The only conflict we had came when, on an afternoon after school, we were in the Goodmans' basement watching *Woody*

Woodpecker. On coming downstairs, Darren McGuinness said, in his usual friendly way

— Here nigger nigger nigger . . .

And, for whatever reason, Margaret chose to defend me.

— He's not a nigger, she said.

That brought such mirth from those around us, I wasn't sure whether I should laugh or not. When Margaret ran out to the yard, I didn't know if I should follow or stay in the basement with the others.

I did follow her out, but I was upset that she'd ruined my afternoon.

Aside from that, and aside from the pain I began to feel on being separated from her, our infatuation was good.

It surprises me that I have ever had such uncomplicated feelings for another.

I have not had them since.

Given how long we lived together, how singular her influence has been on my life, I knew very little about my grandmother.

I've mentioned her cooking (Pablum and plum pudding)

> her habits (dandelion wine)
> her intermittent concern for my well-being
> her slovenliness
> her love of poetry . . .

She fed me, provided a home of sorts, did what she could for me in her lucid moments, and did no irreparable harm in her moments of abandon. For me, these were the things that mattered. Everything else only clouded the issue.

If she couldn't quite love me, that wasn't entirely her fault. Besides, despite all that passed between us, I loved her. How could it be otherwise? For ten years, what tenderness I knew, infrequent though it was, came from her.

When she died, I was heartbroken.

I would have realized she was dead much sooner, if we'd been a little more affectionate, but we'd evolved a relationship that, while affording us both a great deal of freedom, called for very few words.

It was understood, once I was old enough, that I would go shopping for such things as she wrote on a list pinned to the corkboard in the kitchen. If she planned to cook anything more elaborate than macaroni and cheese, she might let me know, so that I could be home in time to have it warm. (Not always a pleasure.)

In general, she made elaborate meals only for those of her old friends who still came around. Her own meal of choice was bologna sandwiches with radish salad. So food did not bring us together.

Neither did housework.

Although *she* was untidy, I wouldn't have dared to leave my clothes about or my dishes unwashed. My grandmother was strict about whose confusion she wanted to see; it would have been *lèse-majesté* for me to clean up after her. So, I kept my few belongings (books, clothes, comics, and shoes) neat and in place in my room, and left the rest of the house as I found it.

It bored me to stick around, waiting for the disaster of smells, dishes, and newspapers to bring her to herself so that she would tidy up and begin her cycle again.

I wonder how she passed the time. What did she think about, for all those hours on end? Did she live the coming of her own death? She must have felt as lonely as I did, but perhaps she imagined her solitude differently, giving it escarpments and a platinum moon.

Whatever it was she thought, she died in 1967.

It was a Friday in April; a Friday, because there was no school the next day, no hour by which I had to be in bed. I had saved fifteen cents for the latest *Fantastic Four*, which I would have to sneak into the house, so much did my grandmother dislike comic books.

I had come directly home from school, to pick up the empties I'd saved, and then tried to sneak out again, noiselessly.

The clinking of the bottles disturbed my grandmother. She said

— Thomas, is that you, dear?

(Her last words, as far as I know.)

— Yes, I answered.

From the store, I went to the school yard and read my comic. I'd have returned home after that (comic book rolled around my leg, tucked into my sock, hidden by my pant leg), but the girls were skipping in the Goodmans' driveway, and Margaret asked me to be an ender.

It was only after turning rope for an hour or so that I went home.

My grandmother was still in her armchair, facing the television. The television was on, tuned to *Let's Sing Out*. I made myself a peanut butter and jam sandwich for supper. And then, quietly as I could, I snuck to my room.

Once I'd made it safely, I called out

— I'm going to read, Gran . . .

and lay on my stomach, on my narrow bed, and reread every frame of *The Fantastic Four*.

To keep myself from reading the comic again, and exhausting it too soon, I must have taken up something my grandmother would not have been upset to see: Dumas, Dickens, or Defoe. And, as often happened on Fridays, I read myself to sleep. (I distinctly remember thinking how strange it was that my grandmother had watched *Let's Sing Out.* "Caterwauling" was a thing she hated.)

The next morning, I woke to the sound of the television tuned to a station that hadn't begun to broadcast. My grandmother was in her armchair, but, from where I stood, she was sitting strangely: she had straightened up, her back no longer touching the back of the chair.

— Morning, Gran, I said.

She didn't answer, but that wasn't unusual. If she'd been drinking, it was natural for her to ignore me. I sensed something wrong, though. For one thing, she smelled a little stronger than usual. I thought at first there was something spoiled in the fridge, but the kitchen smelled better than the living room. That in itself was odd.

— Gran? I said.

Still no answer, and I thought: I'm not talking to you either, then.

I made myself a margarine sandwich, drank a glass of orange juice, and went outside to play in the garden. An idea wouldn't leave me alone, though: *Let's Sing Out* ... and the strong smell ... and ...

And what?

I looked halfheartedly for centipedes, distractedly admired the buds on the neighbor's willow, but it was as if I'd misplaced something valuable.

Then, all of a sudden, I knew what had been missing: the sound of her breathing. Instead of the labored drawing in and noisy letting out, there had been silence, a silence under the silence. I can't express my relief at having remembered the missing thing.

I went back inside.

— Gran, I said. Are you going out today?

No answer.

I took the unprecedented step of turning her television off and, listening intently, heard nothing, exhilarated that I was right: no sound, the only breath my own.

I was almost giddy with relief. I wanted to say: Look, Gran, you're not breathing!

Her eyes were open; she was looking toward the television, but above it, to a spot on the wall.

I touched her arm.

It was at that moment I had my first hint of disaster. Where was I to go? Whom should I call? What should I say?

My first and most comforting thought was of Mrs. Schwartz. I could tell her all this without panic, and she wouldn't accuse me of anything. I was beginning to feel guilt, to feel that I was responsible for whatever my grandmother had endured.

But the Schwartzes weren't home. I knocked at their door for a very long time.

That left only the Goodmans, if I wanted to speak to adults I knew relatively well, and this was a thing for adults, for front doors. It was possible Mrs. Goodman would answer. That wouldn't be so bad.

Mr. Goodman answered.

— What is it? he asked.

— I think my gran is dead.

— What's that?

— I think my gran is dead.

— Is this some kind of prank?

— No, sir.

— How do you know she's dead?

— She isn't breathing.

— You're sure she isn't breathing lightly?

— Yes, sir.

— All right, all right. I'll be over in a few minutes.

He closed the door and I went back home, having nowhere else to go.

It was only then, having done what I was supposed to do, that I felt a little frightened being in the same house with my grandmother's body. On discovering she was dead, I'd had something to do: tell someone. But that had only made matters worse, as if telling had finished her off. Now I was alone with her corpse and with my own thoughts, which were more disturbing as the minutes passed.

I didn't know where to sit, or where to stand. The kitchen was too close to the living room. The basement was even more frightening than the living room, and though my own room was a small refuge, it was too far from the front door to hear anyone knock.

I went from the kitchen to my room, from my room to the kitchen, unable to decide where to stay. In my bedroom, I made fitful attempts to read, but I was too distracted to care about Crusoe or d'Artagnan. In the kitchen, I sat listening for a knock at the door. The sounds of the house, sounds I'd known all my life, frightened me.

When I was in the kitchen, I wanted to be in my room. When I was in my room, I wanted to be in the kitchen. Not once did it occur to me to go outside.

It wasn't that I was afraid of my grandmother's body, you

understand. It was that I couldn't stop thinking about it, and time passed slowly, and Mr. Goodman took hours to knock.

Three days later, my grandmother was buried.

I remember her funeral, but only vaguely. There were very few people at St. Philip's Church, most of them old, almost all of them women.

— Oh yes, mm hm, she was quite a woman was Eddy.

— Not to say she didn't have a temper.

— We all have that, dear . . . no worse than any one of us, I daresay.

— Better than some . . . better than some.

— Are you sitting to the left of the casket, Dorothy? I'll sit with you.

The church was dim, as churches always are in my memory; tall white candles on the altar, small brown coffin between the banks of pews; incense, candle wax, and, because I was sitting next to Mrs. Schwartz, patchouli.

It was hushed, as churches are, so that every cough and sniffle sounds, then echoes, along with every creak of the benches and the rustle of hymnals.

"O God, Our Help in Ages Past" flared briefly and went quickly out, there being so few voices to carry it.

When the service was over, six men, not one of whom I'd ever seen before, carried my grandmother's coffin from the church to the hearse, and it was gone.

I don't much remember the burial. I was there. The coffin was lowered, the first handful of dust was thrown in after it, but I remember all that less than I remember the church, the six men in dark suits, and the smell of incense.

I don't think of those as my last moments with my grandmother.

Her death and her funeral, at both of which she was partially present, were not *our* moments. Our last moment, if there is such a thing as a last moment, came a week later when she was not there at all.

I was staying with the Schwartzes, sleeping uneasily in Irene's room. After a week, I needed more clothes and wanted my comics, so I returned to my grandmother's house.

The house looked almost foreign to me. There was no light, the drapes were all closed, everything waiting for my grandmother's return. I was almost as intimidated, alone in the house, as I had been on the day of her death.

I didn't plan to look into my grandmother's bedroom. It was a room I'd been forbidden to enter. I hadn't seen the inside of it for so many years, I'd forgotten what it looked like.

And yet, on this second venture into what had been my home, I felt something of the bond I had with what was, after all, the only house I'd ever truly known.

My grandmother had regularly assured me that my stay was temporary, that I would be taken to my "rightful home" as soon as my "wretched" mother returned for me, but I was beginning to dread my rightful home, wherever it might be, and I longed for this: a house that was not mine and not quite not-mine. Aside from this house, my own room, my clothes, the books my grandmother had given me and those my grandfather had left, I had nothing at all.

All that to say I felt bereft.

I hesitated before going into her room, worried my grandmother would catch me, but when I pushed the door open, I found a tidy place that smelled of lavender. The bed, with its powder-blue quilt, was neatly made. There was not much dust. There was none of the disarray I expected.

It was as unlike my grandmother as I could imagine.

To one side of the room's only window, a simple rectangular mirror hung above a chest of drawers. The window faced Grove Street. On the chest of drawers was a photograph, in a silver frame, of my grandmother when she was younger. Beside her, with his arm around her waist, was a tall, handsome man wearing black-rimmed glasses and a long overcoat: my grandfather. This was the first time I saw an image of him.

There was a closet in the wall opposite her bed, its white louver doors not quite closed. Half of the closet was given over to versions of my grandmother's two dresses; beneath the dresses were two pairs of nondescript black shoes and an umbrella I'd never seen before, a lacquered wood sphere for its handle. The other half of the closet was taken up by a number of dark suits, beneath which were two brown shoes, in either one of which I could have fit both my feet.

The closet smelled of camphor.

On the wall opposite the window, there was a short, wide bookshelf. It was lined with math books, hymnals, piano music, and books for children: *The Wind in the Willows*, *Alice in Wonderland*, *Gulliver's Travels* . . .

The room was enchanted.

I looked again at the chest of drawers and decided, since it could do no harm, to peek into them, just a look to see.

In one of the drawers there were underclothes. Another was empty. The last one was filled with an assortment of things: a spinning top, a ring, address books, string, coins from another country, a magnifying glass, dollars, and, beneath all that, a handful of photographs and a bundle of letters held together with a red elastic band.

The photos were of my grandfather, of him alone or with my grandmother.

The letters, none in an envelope, were to my grandmother. They were from my mother. The first was written in 1961, when I was four; the last in February 1967. My grandmother had saved them, *that* I understood, but why had she kept them from me?

I lay down on my grandmother's bed, books, letters, photographs, coins, and magnifying glass spread out before me. I read my mother's letters, bored by anything that didn't mention me. I used the magnifying glass to inspect the pictures of my grandfather, to inspect the new illustrations I found in familiar books. And I so forgot myself that I fell asleep in my grandmother's room, on her blue quilt.

I don't know if one ever forgives oneself for what others have done to you. It has taken me so long to forgive my grandmother, I haven't had time for myself, but I like to think I slept beside her in that room, in her arms even, as we'd done before I was five, and that we were both forgiven, each by each, whatever it was I had done.

Fourteen days after my grandmother's death, my mother returned. She had only one thing on her mind, one thing to do: take me with her.

Katarina arrived in a beige four-door something or other, accompanied by a bearded man with missing teeth, Pierre Mataf.

I don't know how she heard her mother was dead, or how she knew where I was staying, but I feel Mrs. Schwartz's concern for me behind my mother's return. The car pulled up in front of the Schwartzes' on a weekday, before Irene and I left for school, just after Mrs. Schwartz had gone to work.

She knocked at the door. I answered.

— Yes?

In a soft voice, the first word I heard her speak, she said

— Thomas?

and leaned forward to hold me. Though it was unpleasant, I allowed myself to be enveloped.

— We have to go, she said.

I knew it was my mother, don't ask me how.

— Home? I asked.

— Somewhere, she answered.

I had a moment to say good-bye to Irene. It didn't occur to me that I might never see her again (I have), that I might never see Mrs. Schwartz again (I likely never will). I took my clothes and my comics.

From my grandmother's house we took an ancient suitcase from the basement and filled it with underwear, shirts, pants, socks, shoes. I wanted to take my favorite books.

— Not too many, my mother said. We'll come back for the rest.

It was difficult to choose, but I took *A Wonder Book*, *The New Arabian Nights*, and, because I couldn't think of leaving Jim Hawkins behind, *Treasure Island*.

Before we left, I proudly showed her the things I'd found in my grandmother's room. I thought it would please her to see the pictures of her father.

— Isn't that your dad? I asked.

She took the photographs from me and looked at each one briefly.

— Yes, she answered.

With my belongings in the suitcase, we went out to the car. Pierre Mataf got out.

— C'est ça ton fils? Il est pas p'tit pantoute . . .

— Just open the trunk, my mother said.

And then, to me

— Into the backseat, Thomas.

— Can we say good-bye to the Goodmans?

— We don't have time.

— But don't you want to say good-bye to Mrs. Schwartz?

— Who?

— Lillian Schwartz?

— Never heard of her, Thomas.

It was only then I began to doubt the identity of the woman who'd come for me. How casually she'd discarded the photographs of her father; how quickly she'd quit her childhood home.

I realized my mistake as we were on the road to Orangeville. I had asked if she wanted to say good-bye to Lillian *Schwartz*. As we drove past yet another small town, I asked

— Don't you remember Lillian Martin?

It wasn't possible, for me, that Lillian's version of their childhood should be a fabrication; inconceivable, but a source of anxiety nonetheless.

— Who?

— Lillian Martin . . . your best friend?

— I don't know what you're talking about, Thomas. My best friend drowned years ago.

— Je savais que t'apportais d'la mauvaise chance, toi, said Mr. Mataf.

— Comment est-ce qu'on dit "bugger off" en français?

— Ah . . . en vrai français c'est "Allez vous faire enculer, madame," mais . . .

— Je comprends la langue française, I said.

— Tant mieux, said Mr. Mataf.

Petrolia evaporated from my consciousness on the very day I left, but it resolutely persists in memory. I closed my eyes when I saw Margaret in the Goodmans' driveway and kept them closed until Reeces Corners.

It was thirty years before I saw Petrolia again, but even before I returned, I think I could have made a credible list of the things I lost:

- My grandmother
- First infatuation, a ten-year-old with a pixie cut and brown eyes
- A small room, a narrow bed, a window onto the Schwartzes' backyard
- Dozens of comic books
- The woods in summer (smell)
- The woods in spring (sound)
- Fields full of: (flora:)   thistles, milkweeds, chicory . . .

     (fauna:)   monarchs, grasshoppers, crickets, ladybugs, shrews, moles, frogs, turtles, thousands of caterpillars, millions of ants . . .
- The smell of the bakery

- The hair tonic at Kells (and the white drape tucked in tight enough to strangle)
- The arena, the exhibition, cows . . .
- A community to which, despite myself, I almost belonged

Thousands and thousands of impressions out of which I could rebuild a version of the place, in three dimensions, from gate to gate.

Geography

V

Erratic. I've been erratic lately.

I've been spending so much time in the past, it's difficult to return to the present for bread and libraries. I have been absorbed by memories of Katarina and Henry, and have become more lenient with myself.

7 o'clock:	I am awakened by the alarm and perform such duties as must be performed to begin the day (defecation, abstersion, depilation).
9 o'clock:	I write, with a break to feed Alexander and to clean house.
11 o'clock:	I continue writing, with an eye to a noontime pause in the action for (a light) lunch: celery.
1 o'clock (P.M.):	I write my letters to the *Citizen*, which, frankly, never took much time and now takes almost none. I have to scour its pages to find anything commendable, or objectionable. These days my heart just isn't

in it, but I persist because it is a connection to the outside world and to the kind of misery that puts my own in perspective.

3 o'clock (P.M.): I go over what I've written, and then set out for the library or for a long walk. (It doesn't matter where I walk or how far. These days I walk in your company.)

5 o'clock (P.M.): I return from the library and read. I read anything at all, and eat.

7 o'clock (P.M.): I continue to read, but something other than what I was reading at 5. So if, from 5 to 7, I were reading a biography, say, then for the next two hours I'll take up a book of poetry or history. Yesterday, for instance, I began at 5 with Smith's biography of Robert Graves. (It reminded me of Henry.) At 7, I carried on with *The Phenomenology of Mind* (Bailie, trans.) (It also reminds me of Henry, with its dark night in which all cows are black, but the great charm of this book is that, though I'm reading it in English, it feels as if I were understanding it in German, a language I don't understand at all.)

9 o'clock (P.M.): I feed Alexander, again, and bathe, again. (If you'll have me at all, my love, you shall have me clean.)

11 (P.M.) to 7 (A.M.): Sleep.

Wandering in the past, returning to feed Alexander . . .

There's a Cartesian smudge on all this, isn't there? Mind in the past, body in the present? Yet, I prefer to think that when I write of the past my body is back there with me.

It's like those dreams you have when a clock is ringing and, in your dream, you turn it off, wake up, shower even. All the while you hear a mysterious sound like a bell, or like a telephone, or like the cry of a small child. And then, suddenly, perhaps in the midst of your shower, you realize it's the sound of your own alarm clock, that you're still asleep, though the shower was wonderful, and there was bacon cooking, and the sun was up over the city of your dreams.

All of you is in that dream, your mind and your body. Both of them must come back to turn off the alarm, to get up. Just so, both of them must return from the past for me to feed Alexander.

I prefer this idea to one that has part of me suffering in 1967, while the rest of me molders here, thirty years later.

I wouldn't want you to think I spend a lot of time reading philosophy. Philosophy is only one step away from poetry, where private worlds are concerned, and it makes me almost as uncomfortable. Were it not for Henry, I wouldn't be reading Hegel at all.

Still, I was reading Hegel, and the ancient Greeks came up, as they always do, and it occurred to me that Heraclitus and Parmenides would have made miserable travelers.

For Heraclitus, all is in flux. You can never step into the same river twice; no permanence except the permanence of change and becoming. What a dire thing travel becomes when home won't persist. Once you go away, you can never return. "What price Florida?" you'd wonder.

But really, in the Heraclitean scheme of things, even as you sit within it, home changes. No sleep, no rest, no blindness, no stasis can keep home home, so you might as well go.

For Parmenides, on the other hand, change is the illusion. All is one, and there can be no movement, no becoming, no variety that is not a delusion of the senses. Travel is impossible. The only thing that persists is home. "Whither Florida?" you'd ask. And what a drab and desperate situation that would be. You'd thank God for your five senses, which, though they deceive, make travel possible . . .

This is just the kind of speculation Henry would have loved, but what I'm trying to say is that I sometimes have as much trouble knowing where I am in Place as I do in Time.

That's a failing in one who's trying to tell you about himself, I know, but I hope it isn't insurmountable.

The province through which I traveled with my mother and Mr. Mataf is difficult to pin down.

I haven't seen all of it, of course; so much is only accessible to beavers. I've passed through the north of the province, on my way to small conferences in Gimli and Moosonee, and was amazed by the huts, houses, Ski-Doos, and decrepit stations hidden behind such mysterious names as Timiskaming, Obatanga, Batchawana Bay, Central Patricia, Sioux Lookout, Kashabowie . . .

In my experience, though, the north and the south could share a motto:

Ontario: *Where You're Ever Close to Water*

Which is appropriate for a province that looks like a fish with its head cut off:

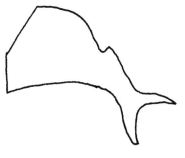

figure 1

(Or like a fish with its head in Manitoba's mouth.)

There are so many lakes, ponds, rivers, streams, rivulets, freshets, creeks and cricks . . . more water than can fit on a map. It's as if one had only to take two steps in any direction to swim, to fall through thin ice, to drown.

That isn't quite the way it felt, driving through Southern Ontario in 1967. There was a great deal of water, but what I especially remember are boulders, rocks, earth, and trees, those and the inexplicable relationship of my mother and Mr. Mataf, its short scope.

VI

From the moment we left Petrolia, my small world splintered.

I was with two strangers, in the back of a car that smelled of cigarettes; and because I was with strangers, every physical detail was important as a clue to my place.

In April 1967, I was my mother's son, but "son" was too abstract an idea. I had never been a "son" as such. I was "Thomas MacMillan," but what use was that to me? None of the details that added up to Tom MacMillan had any real significance for my mother or Mr. Mataf.

If I had been the right kind of youth, if I had been outward and gregarious, I might have used this confusion to set the foundations of the relationship I wanted. With nothing given, there was opportunity to participate in my own definition. At that moment, in the automobile driving east, so much was possible.

Still, though they didn't know me, and I was unsure who Thomas MacMillan was, I brought with me things that made it difficult to set any kind of foundation. I brought with me ten lonely years, a habit of deferring to potentially violent people, a self-protective quiet, and overdeveloped powers of observation; none of them qualities to help one act in the world. Just the opposite. I brought with me things that made action a last resort.

Besides, it was all I could do to decide how to interpret my mother's behavior.

You know, in those moments I didn't resent her, I loved my mother. I have seen her happy, sad, considerate, inconsiderate, loving, and vengeful, but I've never been entirely certain how to interpret her words or her behavior.

That wouldn't be so odd, if the rest of the world had had similar difficulties, but I've known men who could play her like an instrument, men who couldn't, or simply wouldn't, see her convolutions, and these were the very ones who seemed to have her love and attention.

I still wonder if my mother wasn't puzzling to me alone; though, in my defense, I suspect she was deliberately eccentric when I was around.

I remember that, sometime after I left home, we were sitting in her living room talking about praying mantises. It was gardening season. She never failed to ask me about insects in the spring, either how to get rid of them or, in the case of mantids, how best to use them.

I was at one end of her new, white-cushioned sofa. Without missing a beat in the conversation, she got up, went into the kitchen, returned with a jar of raspberry preserve and a spoon, and deliberately dribbled a spoonful of jam onto the cushion beside me.

I assumed this was her way of disagreeing with me, so I changed the subject, suggesting that, perhaps, weed killer might be best for a garden as small as hers. And, before you knew it, we were off on the subject of chemicals.

Over the next two weeks, whenever I visited, I avoided mentioning the sofa and, naturally, sat elsewhere than on the stain.

By pure chance I was with her when the serviceman from Capital Cleaners came in to "wet clean" the upholstery. It was then I discovered my mother had won, a month earlier, a free cleaning in a raffle, the first thing she'd won in her life. But as most of her furniture was then new, the prize was useless without some sort of stain.

Perhaps if I'd asked, she might have told me why she was spilling raspberry preserve on her new cushion. But it seems I never learned how to ask my mother the right question at the right time. If I'd asked why she was spilling jam on the sofa, she'd have answered with something like

— I forgot our dessert, sweetheart.

For some reason, she thought me too serious to be taken seriously.

Along with my mother, there was Mr. Mataf to consider. My first, apprehensive, thought was that he might be my father.

My apprehension had most to do with his appearance. He was, to my ten-year-old self, vinegary beyond words. To begin with, he was missing one of his front teeth *and* the incisor beside it. He was unshaven; he wore a buckskin jacket with fringed sleeves, and his skin was lighter than mine. He couldn't have been much taller than I was then (five feet), because I distinctly remember being unable to avoid his breath whenever we were face-to-face; it smelled of wet dog. And, because I'd announced that I understood French, he spoke to me often enough. I did understand French, but I'd never had occasion to hear its Quebec variation, a wash of new words and almost familiar sounds. I had to pay particular attention to him when he spoke.

Whenever we stopped to eat, or to replenish the radiator, or to wait for the motor to cool, he would rub my head and ask

— Ça va, p'tit?

and look over at my mother. He was so obviously uncomfortable with me, I wondered why he didn't rub her head and leave me out of it.

— Il parle pas beaucoup, ton fils.

— So . . . ?

— Arrache-moi pas la tête, shit. J'fais juste remarquer, c'est tout.

— Who's tearing your head off?

— Tu sais c' que je veux dire . . .

There were a number of things wrong with Mr. Mataf's car. The worst was a slow leak in the radiator that obliged him to stop regularly to let the car cool down or to refill the radiator. Nor did the car's headlights work, and this had as conspicuous an effect on our odyssey as the radiator. We drove along back roads, avoiding cities (well, London, Kitchener, and Guelph). We didn't travel at night.

We were often becalmed. This was mostly dull, sometimes interesting.

The first day out was warm. I filled my pockets with stones from the side of the road and, when the adults needed to talk, I wandered about the side of the road, throwing stones in whatever water I found or at skinny birches.

My mother and Mr. Mataf needed to talk, or wanted to be alone, quite a bit. Selfish, they were, and if I'd been closer to either of them, or a little less used to being on my own, it would have been painful. As it was, the stones and trees, toadstools and ferns were just enough to keep me occupied. Occasionally, not too often, I would hide behind the rocks or trees until one, or both, of them came looking for me. I thought this daring, because I wasn't sure they'd come for me at all.

Still, the really interesting moments came when I returned to the car after a period of exploration. Sometimes Mr. Mataf was visibly angry. Sometimes my mother was quiet. At times they were calm, at others agitated. At times they were, one or the other, or both, happy or relieved or, at least, inclined to speak sweetly to me.

We stopped often enough, between Petrolia and Orangeville, for me to anticipate the shifts in mood between the moment I was told (by Mr. Mataf)

— Va-t-en voir s'il y a des chevaux dans la fôret . . .

and the moment I was called back in, though I couldn't predict what the mood would be at my return.

When I was with them, they communicated with insults or jests or half sentences that meant nothing to me.

— Je me doutais . . .

— De quoi?

— Chut!

— Quoi chut?

— We don't have to talk about that now.

— T'es pas sérieuse.

— Ne vous fâchez pas, Monsieur Mataf.

— Fallait bien que je me fâchasse un jour.

— What?

Each of those syllables, or syllables like them, had meanings that depended on a host of details:

Was his hand on her shoulder?   *Was her hand on his?*
Was his hand on her knee?   *Was her hand on his?*
What was his tone of voice?   *What was hers?*

Was there laughter at the beginning of a sentence? At its end?
Was such and such said at a stoplight, or on the open road?

It was impossible for me to keep all that in mind.

In a way, it was easier for me to tell what was going on from outside the car. That was like watching animals in a cell: soundlessly (from my vantage), they gesticulated, opened and closed their mouths, scratched their heads, seemed to vibrate when angry or slacken when relaxed. This wordlessness (from my vantage) was less recondite than their verbal exchanges.

I now realize that, that day, on the way to Orangeville, which was a step toward Montreal, I was witness to one of the final days of a relationship. I would have to have been much older to reconstruct their affair from what were, essentially, its embers, but it appeared to me, on our first day, that my mother was the more loving, that Mr. Mataf couldn't possibly love her, that he was impatient with things as they were.

And up to a point, I was right.

In all the years I knew her, my mother most often loved men who, whatever their feelings for her, were not inclined to stick around. As far as I'm concerned, that was the only charm most of them possessed.

At times, I blamed myself for their departures, but a pattern is a pattern, and it was my mother's. I don't think she was masochistic. Only one of the men who left her was physically abusive, and she was glad to see that one go.

This opens an unpleasant subject, but I must admit I have no idea if my mother was sexually masochistic or not. That's a strange thing to suggest about one's mother, and mine is so recently dead . . . but this veil over our parents' sexuality (for which I'm grateful, don't misunderstand me) hides an aspect of love, the physical, that one unconsciously learns from them, don't you think?

Then again, moving backward from myself to my mother, it is possible that my own lack of interest in being bound and whipped is proof that she had no interest in it either . . . *requiescat in pace*.

In any case, on the subject of my mother and Mr. Mataf, the pathos of their "final days" loses its poignancy when one knows that this particular man was one in a line of similar men.

It was soon clear that my mother and Mr. Mataf were traveling without much money.

The implications of being without money were still a little murky to me. I mean, my grandmother, while denying me much, never scrimped on the things she felt I needed: woolen long johns, clothes so sturdy they stood up on their own, shoes fresh from the cow, and nutritious foods like Pablum and bran, bran and Pablum.

I certainly wanted frivolous things. I wanted skates and bicycles, but I didn't miss them.

It was this trip that taught me some of the miseries of indigence. No, that sounds too dramatic. The miseries I experienced were less than epic, but they've stayed with me.

We had stopped in Lucan, for gasoline, when Mr. Mataf said

— Viens-t-en toi. On va se promener un peu.

I thought he wanted to walk around the station, a little something to stretch our legs, but we crossed the street and went into a restaurant.

The restaurant smelled of kerosene. It was dimly lit, with counter and stools to one side, booths to the other. To the right of the front door, behind the first booth and partially hidden from the counter by a spin-a-rack of books, there was a red Coca-Cola cooler.

— Tom, va chercher trois Cokes, et amène-les à ta mère.

— Okay.

— 'Ey you dere, 'ow mush for da Coke? Mr. Mataf asked the man behind the counter.

— How many?

As he went to the counter, I took three of the emerald-glass bottles from a pyramid in the belly of the cooler and carried them to my mother as he'd asked.

My mother was suspicious of the offering.

— Where did you find these?

— Mr. Mataf got them for you.

— I see.

She kept quiet until Mr. Mataf returned, paid for the gas, and drove us out of Lucan.

— Thank you for the drink, she said darkly. Whose money did you spend?

But Mr. Mataf was in a good mood.

— Il est bien 'andy, ton fils . . .

(He was handy himself. He was the first man I ever saw open a bottle with his teeth. Not that I've sought them out since.)

— You used our money to pay for these?

— Oui, mais j'ai pas payé pour toute. J'ai payé pour *une* seulement.

— And how did you manage that?

— Je t'ai bien dit qu'il était 'andy, ton fils. Il a pris trois Cokes sans que Monsieur Tête Carrée l'aie vu, puis ensuite . . . ensuite, t'aurais du me voir . . . Le monsieur derrière le comptoir, il pensait que c'était avec des frogs qu'il avait affaire. Ça j'lai compris tout'd'suite, et je me suis dit: Okay d'abord tu va en avoir des frogs toi. J'ai fait semblant de ne rien comprendre, mais pas un mot! Il répétait, "'Ow many? 'Ow many?" puis moi, "'Ow mush? 'Ow mush?". . .

Mr. Mataf was pleased with himself.

— Ça commençait à l'agacer. Alors, j'ai dit, mais lentement, "'Ow . . . mush . . . for . . . ha . . . Coke . . . for . . . da . . . boy?" Là il a embarqué. Il criait, "Ten cents! Ten cents!" Il me criait ça en face, "Ten cents! Ten cents!" Okay, mister. J'ai sortit mon argent et j'ai laissé dix sous noirs. "T'ank . . . you . . . very . . . mush" que j'ai dit. Il était pas mal heureux de me voir du dos, celui-là. T'aurais du voir la face qu'il avait.

They were in fits, both of them, by the end of the story. I didn't see anything funny in it, though. It all amounted to Mr. Mataf using me to steal two bottles of Coke, and though I'd stolen one or two small things in my life, I'd been led to believe theft was wrong.

It *was* wrong, in my little world.

In the real world, the bottles of Coke were our lunch, though we drank them before noon, and there was nothing between them and the ham sandwiches we ate for supper.

After our first day together, I didn't know my mother a great deal more than before we met.

No, that's not true, but what did I know?

I knew how she looked. That's not negligible. Her skin was darker than mine; her nose wasn't as flat. She was thin, and her hair, unruly and long, was more or less constrained by a brightly colored, beaded hair band. To the left of her mane, just along her neck, there was a dark mole. From my place in the car, directly behind her, it was the distinguishing mark I saw most.

I suppose my mother was pretty, though when I close my eyes to picture her face as a young woman, it's difficult to keep in mind. (Her face is all the faces she has had in Time, from the moment I first saw her to the moment she turned away from me and died.) She wasn't what I had expected. Her voice was lower. She wasn't warm and loving, and we didn't take to each other right away.

Worse, there was something in the way she carried herself, something in her gestures, that suggested my grandmother.

Above all, there was self-control; self-control even when she lost control. She never raised her voice, never showed the outward signs of panic, even in panic. You'd have called her level-headed, but for the fact

a) she'd abandoned her child
b) she'd never visited, though she'd written as if she might have liked to
c) she returned for her only child two weeks after her mother's death, but penniless in the company of a penniless man who seemed not to like children
d) she returned in a car on the verge of collapse.

And that's only a partial list of what, from here, look to be signs of recklessness. It might have been easier, for me, if her instability had been more obvious. On our first day, the only moment she lost composure came when she ate. I could see the effort she made to control herself as she bit into her half of our ham sandwich. She devoured it, and then opened the window for a breath of air.

I thought her bad-mannered. I ate slowly.

———

We stopped with the coming sunset, just outside of Orangeville, by the side of a dirt road, beside a flooded field, the nearest farmhouse some distance away.

It must have taken us about eight and a half hours to go from Petrolia to Orangeville, 160 kilometers away, stopping every half hour or so for fifteen to twenty minutes; the equivalent, as I reckon it, of 5.6 hours waiting against 2.8 hours traveling, and a mean speed of just over 57 kilometers/hour along pebbled back roads, beside flooded fields, barns for Someone and Son, cows, horses, dung.

We ate our bits of sandwich in silence, drank warm water from the bottles Mr. Mataf had filled at a gas station. It was the first time I drank water that smelled of eggs. Then, the adults got out of the car and took a small tent from the trunk.

— You won't mind sleeping in the car, will you, Thomas?

— C'est pas un enfant, voyons.

— You'll be more comfortable in . . .

— I don't mind.

— Tu vois?

It was still light out as they looked for a bit of dry land on which to pitch their tent. I watched them from the car until the tent was raised and the two of them crawled in.

It looked too small to accommodate them both.

Under the circumstances, it would have been surprising if I'd been able to sleep. I lay down in the backseat, as night came, listening for the sounds of night.

For a frightened child, I was self-possessed.

VII

—

From here, it looks as if the second day with Mr. Mataf, from Orangeville to Marmora, was the real beginning of my life with Katarina.

Though I lived it as a single, chaotic passage, I remember the day as threefold:

1. Hunger
2. Misunderstanding
3. Night

1 Hunger

I hadn't slept, or I'd drifted in and out of sleep.

The dark had intimidated me. The stars that, on other occasions, I've been thankful for refused to become the constellations I loved. I might have found Orion if I'd wanted, but I didn't want. It was cold and I had no cover, save for my jacket and a sweater I found on the floor.

By morning, the air was like sand in my mouth. There was a fog on the road, and the sky was gray. (I've always disliked fog.) And I was hungry.

Naturally, wishing for the reappearance of my mother and

Mr. Mataf seemed to keep them away. Every minute from sunrise to late morning, when the two of them actually woke, was excruciating. And, when they did get up, it took them forever to crumple and fold their tent, to put it back in the trunk.

It's odd, but nowadays I both love and dislike being hungry. For me, being from a class that disposes of hunger easily, it isn't the soul-destroying thing it is for those whose lives depend on the next bite. For me, hunger is one of the more interesting agreements I have with my body. It begins with an almost pleasant feeling of lack, an awareness of something missing. And this awareness I can ignore, the same way I have, until now, ignored nostalgia. But from this first moment, centered in my innards, the state becomes gradually more general; it goes from being physically insistent to being both physically and intellectually manifest. This is the stage, when I've been hungry for hours, I like best. There's an exhilaration to the beginning of an accord of mind and body. You may be thinking of whatever, the way bare trees look when they're shaken by the wind, for instance, when suddenly these same trees remind you of a whisk whipping cream, of the brushes used to glaze a fish, of broccoli, and if broccoli then salad, and if salad then soup. And once you've thought of soup, and soup is, let's say, the thing you really wouldn't mind eating just now, it's as if you've always had a particular relationship to soup. Soup itself becomes an intellectual proposition, as important in its way as the soul. And what, one wonders, did St. Augustine like to eat? Well, he was from Carthage, so his soups would have been fish-based, fish-based and salty, and how could one possibly understand St. Augustine without knowing this about him? The purpose of all this thinking is, of course, to get me to the kitchen, but when it works and

I do go to the kitchen, I'm inevitably surprised to find myself there, a can of soup in one hand, a can opener in the other. It's a moment of unknowing, of lostness in thought, that brings one back to knowing, back to *the* thought: hunger. From here, if one chooses not to eat, the impulse may vanish, as if to say: Okay, I brought you to the kitchen. It's out of my hands. Don't blame me . . . And off it goes to do its strangest work, disappearing now only to return stronger, more insistent later, turning everything to food, turning food itself to something luminous. I also appreciate this stage of hunger: the feeling of lack isn't yet unavoidable or painful; the conversation between myself and my self has simply grown more heated. It's the beginning of seeing clearly, or seeing intently, and it can last for days, days during which I feel more excitement than pain. Just after this, of course, there's a point when, tired of sending messages you use as entertainment, your body gets on with the business of eating itself, sending signals of alarm occasionally, when it remembers it isn't supposed to do this. That's when I like to eat, if I've been fasting. To go on after that is self-punishment.

Anyway, on the morning I'm speaking of, I was hungry somewhere near the beginning of hunger, but I was too young to savor it . . .

They had been arguing.

Mr. Mataf was annoyed. He grumbled his way through key finding, car starting, and taking off. My mother asked how I'd slept.

— I'm hungry, I said.

— Your son is 'ungry, said Mr. Mataf.

(It sounded as if I were "angry.")

— I heard him.

— Alors, on va faire quelque chose ou . . .

— I'm hungry, I said again.

And I began to cry, need having shown me the tragic in my situation: alone with strangers, far from the only home I'd ever known, unhappy with the woman who was supposed to be my mother, intimidated by the man she was with, cold and uncomfortable from a sleepless night in the back of a car, hungry.

— Okay, toi. On n'a pas besoin d'Hollywood à c't'heure.

And then from my mother

— Don't talk to him that way.

Mr. Mataf let out a stream of invective, with *maudit* this and *maudit* that, *calice*, *hostie*, *tabernacle*, before my mother hit him on the side of the face. (I was going to write "slapped," but I distinctly remember a fist, and the car veering out of its lane and onto the soft shoulder.)

Mr. Mataf may have thought, briefly, of stopping the car to get over his surprise or to strike her, but he didn't. He drove on. And after a while, the only sound the sound of the car itself and the air whistling by, he said

— I'm sorry.

My mother said

— You should be.

I myself had stopped sniffling the moment she hit him. Even I, who had not often been in cars, thought it risky to assault the driver while he was driving, but the violence changed the mood. I was frightened; my mother was calm; Mr. Mataf relaxed.

— Okey doke, MacMillan, cherchons quelque chose à manger.

Not only did he relax, but he became almost cheerful.

We stopped in a small town, Alliston or Bradford, I'd guess. Mr. Mataf parked on a main street, almost deserted though it was midmorning and the sun was out.

— Leave us alone for a minute, please, my mother said to Mr. Mataf.

— Je vous en prie, mademoiselle, he answered.

He got out slowly, stretching as he walked away from the car. My mother turned to me, her face serious.

— Thomas, she said, I'd like you to do something for me.

— Okay . . .

— You know, Pierre and I don't have much money . . . just enough for gas to Montreal . . . and we don't have any food left . . . you understand?

— Yes.

— So . . . when we go into this store, I'd like you to help me take food for us.

— We're going to steal?

— Yes.

— But what should I take?

— Don't take anything too big, and watch out for anyone watching you . . . Take whatever you can, anything you can hold under your shirt.

— Under my shirt? Won't they see it?

— Not if you're careful.

— But what are you going to take?

— Anything I can fit in my purse, she said. Are you sure you want to do this?

— If we have to . . .

Not that I believed it would be so simple. As I said, theft was more or less foreign territory to me, and here it was again, though this was different from the Cokes I'd taken the day before. I had a premonition of disaster.

— Ready? my mother asked.

And I said

— Yes.

(It's odd. I have a vivid memory of all this, but the details sometimes shimmer. Was Mr. Mataf's car really brown? I suddenly remembered it as blue, and just as suddenly it was brown again and the sky is blue, and the street smells of rain, and I'm walking toward the store with my hands in my pockets.)

Mr. Mataf was already in the store, talking to the tall man behind the counter.

— Go ahead, my mother whispered.

And I moved away from her, eyes lowered, to case the store. Well, to look for what would fit under my shirt, anyway.

The store was dimly lit. There were three short aisles, along which the shelves were stocked with tins and packages not flat enough to take. There was a refrigerator against the back wall, and in the refrigerator there was bologna and mock chicken, both of them compact enough to steal.

No sooner had I decided what it was I was going to steal than I could feel myself being watched. Mr. Mataf and my mother were both near the front of the store; my mother's purse was open.

The man behind the counter stood by expressionlessly, waiting and, I distinctly felt, watching me closely, though whenever I turned toward him he turned his head away.

The problem was there was no one to distract him. And then, finally, a tall man with a crew cut entered, a distraction for precisely as long as I needed to take a package each of bologna and mock chicken. Before I could think twice, I slipped them under my jacket and shirt, one tucked into my pants in front, the other tucked behind.

How long did it take me? (How long were we in the store, for that matter?) That I don't know at all. I felt exhilarated, embarrassed, proud, and focused on escape, on getting away before one of the packages slipped from my waist.

I almost ran from the store and, as it turns out, I should have run, but there were at least two impediments to flight: first, despite my lack of experience, I knew that running would be an admission of guilt; second, the faster I moved, the more likely I was to lose the luncheon meat. So I moved slowly toward my mother.

— On y va? said Mr. Mataf as I approached.

And I walked with them to the counter, relieved that we were finally going. Mr. Mataf bought a package of gum.

— Do you have anything to mention, Thomas?

My mother was speaking to me, but I didn't understand why. I looked up; three faces looked down at me. The proprietor's face was stern, one eye closed. Mr. Mataf's face was unreadable, blank. My mother looked at me with what seemed to be . . . disappointment.

— No? I asked.

— Are you sure?

— Yes? I answered.

— An' hin your pocket? asked Mr. Mataf.

I've never felt such confusion. They both knew what I'd done, of course, but I thought I'd done it for them. Was it possible I'd so misunderstood her that I'd done the opposite of what my mother wanted? No answer from the expression on her face.

I emptied my pockets, more and more upset as each of my belongings clicked on the countertop: all my money (small change), the key to my grandmother's house, the key to the Schwartzes', a genuine leather wallet . . .

The adults looked on impassively, joined now by the Crew Cut. He looked amused.

— Very good, said the proprietor, now lift your shirt.

I looked up at my mother.

— Go ahead, she said.

The package was there in my waistband.

— I'm ashamed of you, said my mother.

— But you . . .

That was all I managed to say before she slapped my face. (The only time she ever slapped me, except in jest.)

— Please don't talk back.

She turned to the proprietor and gently pushed the package across the counter.

— We're so sorry, she said.

And then, to Mr. Mataf

— Would you please take Thomas back to the car?

I was still stunned from her slap.

— But . . .

— Ça va, ça va, said Mr. Mataf. Ferme ta gueule un peu, Tom.

And he pulled me away from the counter, after casually sweeping my belongings back into my hands.

I didn't know what to do—cry, run, stand still. Small details stood out from their surroundings: the light-brown fringe on Mr. Mataf's jacket, the texture of the wooden floor, the clinking of the chimes as the door opened, the cool of the mock chicken I'd forgotten to return, my mother's words to the proprietor

— I can't thank you enough.

Outside: sunlight, a steeple, mud on the pavement. And then everything was swept away as I began to cry; not whimper, not sniffle. I cried as one cries in dreams, convulsively, breathless, everything in the world, from steeples to sunlight, adding to my despair.

— Mais qu'est-ce que t'as à pleurer de même? asked Mr. Mataf.

And he offered me a stick of gum.

When my mother came back from the store, she said

— Thomas . . . calm down.

I sat in the backseat, inconsolable. And, as we drove slowly from Alliston or Bradford, my mother began to take things from her purse, from Mr. Mataf's jacket: sardines, a tin of condensed milk, a can of soup, peanut butter, crackers . . .

— You were wonderful, she said. That fool was so busy keeping an eye on you, we took everything we needed.

— But why didn't you tell me?

— How could I? Pierre told the man I wanted to teach my son a lesson. He told him you were tricky and he'd have to keep an eye on you. If I'd told you, Thomas, you'd have taken things just to take them. This way, the man saw you were sneaky, and he was so glad to help with your education. I'm sorry . . . Here. This will make you feel better.

She turned around to give me something to eat.

— Really, she said, you were so wonderful it broke my heart.

I couldn't decide whether to eat or go on crying. I believed her when she said it broke her heart, but it was all so unfair.

From here, it still looks unfair; a humiliation I could have done without. Though, when I try to imagine a better plan, I see both her point and her daring. The intimacy of helping a woman with the education of her child must have been irresistible to the man behind the counter.

And it *was* part of my education.

I rarely do what anyone asks me to do without scrupulously thinking it over, and up to now I've avoided beachfront property in the Everglades and coins commemorating the fall of Troy.

So when you have asked me about myself, perhaps it's prudence that has kept me from speaking. (Prudence, reticence, and no idea where to begin.)

I do not think my mother had any of this in mind when she slapped me, but, all the same, her slap is an enduring caution.

2 Misunderstanding

One puts so much stock in the small details of love: a touch on the wrist, a hand on the forehead, a certain inclination of the body, all the signs of yearning in proximity . . .

But the signs of a broken bond are even more revealing: exaggerated inclination, a touch whose violence is hidden in humor

— Mais . . . tu vas pas prendre ça au sérieux . . .

a turning away, sentences unfinished not from blissful and mutual understanding, but from understanding *tout court*.

I mean, if it's in its death rattle that one feels the depth of love, my mother and Mr. Mataf had been in love.

We had stopped to eat and then gone on. The indescribable taste of peanut butter and sardines lingers in my memory.

I don't recall if there were bitter words, but, despite the victory in Alliston (or Bradford), a kind of stress wormed its way into the car.

My mother turned her attention to the passing world, the blue lakes that appeared suddenly and were gone, the watery fields, the fields in which horses, cows, or sheep grazed, and trees, trees, trees, gnarled, thin, and so starved for light they curled around each other.

From time to time, Mr. Mataf said

— On l'a bien eu, celui-là

to no one in particular.

It must have been agony for him to be with two people who found it so easy to keep quiet. He was naturally talkative, demonstrative, gregarious. To make up for the lack of company, he turned on the transistor radio he kept in his pocket and set it on the dashboard.

— Shuger bye, 'onee bunsh . . .

He sang along, sporadically, turning songs I knew into a beautiful near English, improving things like "California Dreamin'" immeasurably, I thought. And, from time to time, he would speak not to me but with me in mind.

— C'est pas si pire, des fois, ton Ontario . . .

or

— Le ciel est si bleu, si calme . . .

On one of our stops to let the radiator cool, he even came out to walk with me, distractedly asking the names for some of the stones by the side of the road.

— C'est quoi ça?

— Schist.

— Pas vrai . . . et ça?

— Limestone . . . talc . . . slate . . .

It must have been a relief for Mr. Mataf to have what could pass for conversation.

— Schist . . . schist . . . talc . . . quartz . . . quartz . . . limestone . . .

— T'as une mémoire vraiment prodigieuse, toi.

And then, because I was embarrassed and because I was curious, I asked

— Où est-ce que vous avez rencontré ma mère?

— Où que j'ai rencontré ta mère? À Vancouver.

— La connaissez-vous depuis longtemps?

— Mais qu'est-ce que c'est tout ça? Un interrogatoire? D'un côté ça fais pas longtemps, d'un aut' ça fais une éternité. La réponse convient-elle à monsieur? Good.

These were the only intimate moments I shared with Mr. Mataf and, to our mutual disappointment, I'd brought up the one thing about which he wanted to be silent.

3 Night

As we'd done the day before, we traveled on narrow roads and small highways from morning until the first sign of sunset.

We stopped near Marmora, by a lake. We ate more of the pilfered groceries, and then, to my surprise, Mr. Mataf left the car, took the tent from the trunk, and set up some distance from the car, alone.

I was alone with my mother.

— I'm going to sleep here tonight, Thomas. I hope you don't mind.

I did mind.

— I don't mind, I said.

It was awkward. There were too many things to say, or too many things to ask. We settled in, she in the front, myself in the back, and we said good night.

It was a cold night, and quiet. I couldn't sleep.

I had been looking up at the moon and the stars for what seemed hours when my mother asked, softly

— Are you sleeping, Thomas?

— No, I answered.

— It'll all be better when we get to Montreal.

— Why are we going to Montreal?

— Well, Pierre knows people there. We'll find work.

— . . .

— It's a wonderful city. I know you'll love it.

— Lillian said you didn't like your mother.

— Lillian seems to have said a lot about me.

— Didn't you?

— Of course I did. I wouldn't have left you with her if I didn't love her.

— What about Lillian? I thought she was your best friend.

— Anne Maurice was my best friend.

— Didn't she drown?

— No, not really.

(What a strange evening it was for Lillian Martin. My mother now admitted her existence, yes, but as an acquaintance. What's more, she admitted she'd spent a night or two with the Martins, yes, but there'd been no swimming, not that she could remember. Yet, despite the contradictions, there are aspects of Lillian's Katarina that make more sense than my mother's versions of herself. It's never been clear who to believe about whom.)

— But why didn't you take me with you?

— I was very young, Thomas. If I'd kept you we'd have had no home, no clothes, no food.

— Couldn't you have stayed in Petrolia?

— No.

— Didn't I have a father?

— Of course you had a father.

— Couldn't he have helped us?

— No, he couldn't.

— Wasn't he a good man?

— Of course he was.

— And you were in love?

— Where do you hear things like that?

— But you were in love?

— Thomas, you're too young to use that word. Really, it's too difficult . . .

(It was dark and quiet. My mother spoke in a near whisper. I wondered if my father were monstrous. Eyeless? Fingerless?)

— Do you love Mr. Mataf?

— I don't know how I feel.

— You don't know if you love someone?

— I don't know if I love Mr. Mataf.

(Of course she loved him. He was her own special misery.)

— What was grandmother like . . . before?

— Mother . . . She was . . . consistent.

— But you loved her?

— Of course I did. She and Father always got along.

— Why didn't you visit us?

— Listen, Thomas, Mother was a capital "B" rhymes with itch, sometimes. After Father died, we didn't get along at all. It would have made things worse if I'd visited.

— How?

— I'd have strangled her to death.

Macabre as it sounds, those were the most reassuring words my mother ever spoke.

We were united in our experience of Edna's ill humor. When we snickered, it was like siblings who dared to call their mother "a bitch."

From then until deep into the night, we exchanged memories of what had been home.

Did I realize the small hole beside my bedroom door was one she'd made with a pencil? And then: a name carved in the baseboard, a broken door, a cracked pot handle, a stain on the kitchen wall . . . all her doing.

If I'd only known where to look, I'd have seen her marks everywhere.

And did she learn to read as early as I, sitting at the kitchen table, sounding out the difficult words: odiferous, complexion, Phoebus? (Yes.)

And did she remember her Lampman? (No, not a word.)

And did I remember my Donne? (Yes.)

Since I am coming to that holy room
Where, with Thy choir of saints for evermore,
I shall be made Thy music; . . .

We said those lines together, and I heard my grandmother's voice as I said them. But it seems it wasn't her poem at all. It had been my grandfather's favorite. My mother heard his voice as she spoke, as Edna must have.

— What was my grandfather like?

— Well, he was tall . . . and he was gentle . . .

— And you loved him?

— I loved him very much.

— Tell me how he died.

— Thomas, it's too late for that now.

We had been talking for hours.

I'd asked my last question on the verge of sleep, and it was like a single question spoken in two worlds. I went from a dark place to a light one, from Mr. Mataf's car to my dream of Mr. Mataf's car.

Here the moon was brighter, and there was a lake nearby, an immense circle on which the moon floated. We had decided to get out of the car, my mother and I, to put our feet in the water, the night was so warm.

The night is always warm, and there are only a few trees between us and the water, and the ground is wet. I hear the soft and familiar words

. . . Anyan, and Magellan, and Gibraltar.

And I'm up to my waist in water.

In the distance there's a white shroud floating on the ripples toward me, and above the shroud are dozens of white moths.

It frightens me to see the moths over water, and then, turning to get out of the lake, I find I can't move.

— I can't move, I say.

But my mother is gone. There is only the lake, the trees, the moon, the moths . . .

I've had this dream so often since, it surprises me that it has a first night. Sometimes, the shroud that floats toward me holds my grandmother's body; her eyes are open beneath the surface of the water, and her mouth moves as she struggles to disentangle herself, or to speak.

At other times, it's my mother's body in the shroud.

In either case, what frightens me are the moths, and the fact that I can't move, that I'm held in the silt beneath the water.

I can't remember who it was beneath the surface that night, Edna or Katarina, but I frightened myself awake and was not at all comforted to find myself still in the place from which I'd awakened.

It was like losing hope.

VIII

For a moment there, remembering Marmora, I was reminded of the shape of our journey, the lay of the land. And it amused me to imagine Southern Ontario as a correlative to my mother's relationship with Mr. Mataf.

I even drew myself a graph:

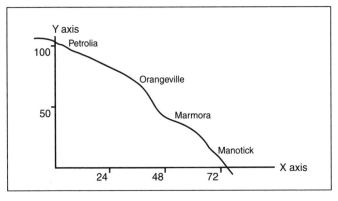

figure 2

The y-axis is Level of Affection.

I don't actually know how "in love" the two of them were at any time, but I assume maximum affection at the point of departure: Petrolia (0, 100).

The x-axis is Time.

Another approximation. I'm not certain what we were doing or where we were at any specific time, but I think it's safe to assume the moment of least affection is Manotick, and it took us some three days to reach: Manotick (72, 0).

No sooner had I finished plotting its points than I began to have serious doubts about my graph. For instance, why not use latitude or longitude for the x-axis?

Ontario begins at around 95° latitude, 42° longitude. It ends around 74° latitude, 56° 51′ longitude. Being able to discriminate between, for instance, 77° 45′ (just before Marmora) and 77° 40′ (just after) would allow for greater precision in finding correspondence between sentiment and the land, wouldn't it?

How wonderful it would be to write

- latitude 77° 45′ — as the sun began its decline on Crow Lake, Pierre Mataf and Katarina MacMillan experienced sadness and a waning of their feelings for each other, emotions both of them would forever associate with the sun's decline on this body of water, on such and such a date, at such and such a time, with a sullen child in tow . . .

- latitude 77° 46′ — . . . the previous sadness gracefully modulated into speculation (by Katarina MacMillan) on their whereabouts, and speculation (by Pierre Mataf) on their final destination on this melancholy evening . . .

My choice of a 24-hour scale (0 to 72) *does* have something vague about it, but the imagination required to write precisely of other people's emotions is quite beyond me. The vagueness of my x-axis is perfectly suited to my memory and imagination, or lack of memory and lack of imagination.

Equally vague is the idea of "affection" I've used for the y-axis. Here, however, emotions of any sort being, by definition, vague, it's clear that precision is likely to create more problems than it solves.

Let's suppose, for instance, that on a more precise scale of the affections

100   equals   "sexual intercourse without resentment"

and that

0   equals   "no sexual intercourse without devastating emotional consequences."

That sounds almost reasonable to me, though its problems are obvious under scrutiny:

1. Is "sexual intercourse without resentment" a suitable definition of the highest sentiment?

   For the sake of argument, and on the principle that outward manifestation of emotion is the most reliable proof we have of the emotions themselves, the answer is an extremely qualified "yes." (For convenience, we leave aside the question of "resentment," whether it must be registered before, during, or after intercourse.)

2. Could my mother and Mr. Mataf have had "sexual intercourse without resentment" in Petrolia?

In all honesty, I don't think so. I can't believe one would break up such a relationship after three days. That is, if they *could* have had unresentful sex in Petrolia, it's highly unlikely they would have separated so soon afterward. They must, then, have been closer to 0 on our new scale than 100. Even so, because emotions often fluctuate wildly (rather than declining steadily, as I have it), it's entirely possible that, either in Petrolia itself or somewhere on its outskirts, they may both have drifted onto that part of the scale that offers tolerable feelings of resentment and makes sexual intercourse a possibility. Imagine, for instance, that they both suddenly remembered their first meeting, first starry night, first passion for each other. A memory like that could push them as high as 50, say, and then all bets are off.

So, our answer is a rather unsatisfying "perhaps."

3. If emotions can fluctuate enough to allow for such intimacy so soon before a final break, can we say precisely when, or even *if*, they fell out of love before their breakup?

No, we cannot, and being unable to answer this particular question makes a mockery of any graph, any plot that includes "affection."

And yet . . .

Though I was inclined to throw my graph away, if only because I wouldn't want you to think I'm hypnotized by geometry, there was something in the gentle fall of the line that was suggestive of the things in simultaneous decline as we made our way across Ontario:

- my mother's relationship to Mr. Mataf
- the version of my mother I'd inherited from Mrs. Schwartz

- my sense of belonging
- my early childhood.

And so, though I hate to misuse graphs, this one was more significant to me as a picture than as a graph *strictu sensu*.

(I often wonder what the contour of our time will be: from the library to a touch, accidental, at the corner of O'Connor and Laurier; our kiss near Lyon, your touch, purposeful, the moon through a window on Percy . . .)

The morning after my dream of a shroud and moths, Mr. Mataf woke us early. He stuffed the tent into the trunk of his car, smartly closed the hood, and slammed the driver's door shut when he got in.

— Okey doke, he said without enthusiasm.

— Trou d'cul, my mother answered softly.

Though the days are generally sunny in my memory, this one is conspicuously wet. Mr. Mataf was wet when he woke us, his jacket mottled. It must have started raining at night. It certainly rained as we drove. I remember a rebuke from Mr. Mataf.

— Ferme-moi cette fenêtre, veux-tu? he said
when I opened a window to put out my hand.

We still stopped to let the engine cool, to fill the radiator, but I spent most of the day in the car, in daytime darkness and turbulent silence.

Though I'd watched them closely for two days, the distaste my mother now had for Mr. Mataf, and he for her, was traumatic for me. I was certain this was all my fault: the silence, the tension, maybe even the weather.

When Mr. Mataf tried to speak to me

— Ça va en arrière?

my mother said

— Leave him alone

making the boundary clear. I was on her side in the skirmish. To speak to me was to speak to her and, as she and he were not speaking, he was not to speak to me.

I'm convinced this was the moment Mr. Mataf abandoned ship. Not that I remember him saying, in so many words, that it was over between them, but that's just it. Being such a spirited man, his lack of response, his silence was the "in so many words." I don't remember him saying another word to my mother, not "good night," not "good-bye." He defiantly spoke to me, though. He said

— Me passerais-tu les biscuits, s'il te plaît

and

— Non, c'est moi qui va dormir dans l'auto ce soir. La tente est pour toi et ta mère

and

— Bonsoir, Tom.

To me, now, the road to Manotick seems like a slow ritual, as if things had to be played out this way, in this theater.

My mother could certainly have soothed Mr. Mataf's feelings, if she'd wanted. The slightest consideration might have brought him back, but she made no effort; not a word to him, after the warning to leave me alone, and very few to me.

Then again, she may have been waiting for an apology, and she had a thing about apologies. I don't quite understand her thinking, but I believe it went like this: "If I'm wrong, I'll apologize, but if I'm wrong and it's obvious to both of us that I'm wrong, then my being wrong is a humiliation and you should apologize to me." (My mother and I, both waiting for an apology, once went two months without speaking to each other.)

I have no idea how Mr. Mataf behaved when they were alone. Perhaps she was entitled to an apology. On the way to Manotick, though, she was so clearly the stronger, I could feel her crush the spirit from him.

Besides the tension and the weather, there was nothing remarkable about the day. It rained and then it stopped.

When it was time to eat, the last tin of sardines was rancid, but the tin of oysters was good. Mr. Mataf said

— Me passerais-tu les biscuits, s'il te plaît?

When we stopped near Manotick[7] for the night, my mother turned to me and asked

— Are you comfortable, Thomas?

Mr. Mataf turned to me and answered

— Non, c'est moi qui va dormir dans l'auto ce soir. La tente est pour toi et ta mère.

He put the car keys in my hand.

My mother immediately got out of the car. It would have

---

[7] I've often wondered how we ended up in Manotick, not only because it's more northerly than one would expect for people on the road to Montreal, but because of the pestilential number of *villes* that afflict the northeastern tail of the province: Frankville, Kemptville, Domville, Stampville, Brouseville, Keelerville, Mainsville, Marvelville, Mayerville, Merrickville, Middleville, Wagarville, Hallville, Orangeville, Innisville, Spencerville, Hainesville, Ellisville, Ramsayville, Marionville, Ettyville, Stanleyville, Chesterville, Maxville, Philipsville, Clydesville, Riceville, Bonville, Bainsville, Mitchellville, Charlesville, Andrewsville, Judgeville . . . There's something almost deliberate about ending up somewhere other than a *ville*. (Well, a *ville* or a *Corners*.)

been beneath her to argue. Instead, she behaved as if it had been her idea the two of us would sleep in the tent rather than the car. It was not raining. We were near the river. She took the things that belonged to us from the car: sweater, food, books.

And when we had dragged the crumpled and sighing mass of tent from the trunk, I gave the keys back to Mr. Mataf.

— Bonsoir, Tom, he said.

This night was even more unusual than the previous, near Marmora.

First, there was the tent, a blue canvas pup, with metal rods for support and wooden pegs for anchor. It was low, and there was scarcely enough room for two. The canvas was damp and smelled of mildew.

It was colder inside the tent than out. We quickly took off our shoes and crawled into the sleeping bag, which was just wide enough for us both.

It was like being trapped with a stranger.

We had already accepted our roles (mother and son) and each had accepted the role of the other, but it was not enough to alleviate the awkwardness. How can I put it? My mother was pretending to be a mother, and her version of "mother" included love of her offspring. I was pretending to be a son, and my version of "son" included a certain ease with my progenitor.

I don't know how she felt, but I had less trouble accepting her as "mother" than I had thinking of myself as "son." My discomfort, the reason I tried to keep absolutely still, was a discomfort with myself as much as it was a discomfort with my mother.

And what did I expect of my mother?

What I expected was the woman I'd built out of the stories I'd heard in Petrolia. I expected a woman unlike my grandmother. I expected Katarina, but my mother obliterated all of that.

The twenty-nine-year-old who said

— Good night Thomas

(and kissed the back of my head) was the person to whom my first ten years led. Everything had to be reinterpreted with her in mind.

My grandmother was different in light of her daughter. The house I'd lived in was different now that I knew the secret signs of Katarina's presence. The town of Petrolia was different because it had driven this woman away (and later called her back). Even recent events changed in significance the more I knew my mother.

The most poignant dilemma that night was how to say "good night." It seemed so important at the time. My mother said

— Good night, Thomas.

What was I to say?

— Good night, Katarina   (?)
— Good night, Mother   (?)
— Good night, Mom   (?)
— Good night   (?)

I said

— Good night.

The following morning, Mr. Mataf was gone.

He'd left our suitcases by the side of the road, but aside from that there was no sign of him.

I rose first, so it was I who called my mother from sleep.

— Mr. Mataf's not here, I said.

My mother got out of the tent. She walked to the side of the road where our suitcases stood, and then, after a moment, unleashed a torrent of language such as I'd never heard from an adult.

— You didn't hear that, Thomas.

I'd felt it, rather.

We stood by the side of the road for what was, in my memory, a very long time, with my mother looking at the river and myself not knowing where to look, until, as if the water had decided for us, we picked up and began walking along the riverside, north.

We left the tent where it was, the sleeping bag unfurled within. My mother carried the suitcases and I tried to keep up to her without complaining.

We walked north, but she didn't tell me *where* we were going. For years I assumed the time she'd spent in silence by the side of the road was time spent trying to decide where to go for refuge, but it may be she was trying to discover an alternative to the river, an alternative to Henry Wing.

Whatever she was thinking, it was a fateful moment in three lives: mine, my mother's, and Henry's.

I can't recall much about the walk to Ottawa. In my version, we walk for hours along the road and the river, and my mother carries our suitcases. When we're hungry she takes the package of mock chicken from her purse and folds the slices onto the last of the crackers.

So I remember it, at least.

The Sciences

The Sciences, Divination: by oracles, *Theomancy*; by the Bible, *Bibliomancy*; by ghosts, *Psychomancy*; by spirits seen in a magic lens, *Cristallomantia*; by shadows or manes, *Sciomancy*; by appearances in the air, *Chaomancy*; by the stars at birth, *Genethliacs*; by smoke from the altar, *Capnomancy*; by currents, *Bletonism*; by the entrails of animals sacrificed, *Hieromancy*; by the entrails of fishes, *Ichthyomancy*; by the entrails of a human sacrifice, *Anthropomancy*; by mice, *Myomancy*; by birds, *Orniscopy*; by winds, *Austromancy*; divination in general, *Mantology*; by a cock picking up grains, *Alectryomancy*; by passages in books, *Stichomancy*; by a balanced hatchet, *Axinomancy*; by meteors, *Meteoromancy*; by numbers, *Arithmancy*; by writings in ashes, *Tephramancy*; by dropping melted wax in water, *Ceromancy*; by sacrificial fire, *Pyromancy*; by fountains, *Pegomancy*; by the dough of cakes, *Crithomancy*; by a balanced sieve, *Coscinomancy*; by dots made at random on paper, *Geomancy*; by pebbles drawn from a heap, *Psephomancy*; by mirrors, *Catoptromancy*; by nails reflecting the sun's rays, *Onychomancy*; by ventriloquism, *Gastromancy*; by the mode of laughing, *Geloscopy* . . .

figure 3
(an abbreviated list of the sciences of divination)

IX

And which to talk about first, the city or Henry Wing? Ottawa has changed so much and so often, I don't know which Ottawa is Ottawa. The city as I first saw it, walking in from Manotick? I barely remember that one. I was tired and miserable. It would have been little more than a convergence of buildings and glass, with a few monuments thrown in.

It's a strange thing to contemplate, strange in the same way meeting my mother was strange, but there was a time I didn't know the Parliament buildings, the Château, the Canal. Perhaps I saw them, coming in from Manotick, but they were not significant to me then and I don't remember.

A great deal of my past is lost through the inattention of my younger selves, but what I miss most are first impressions of certain places.

The Parliament buildings meant nothing to me for years, and then suddenly they did. Now, they persist in my imagination even when I dream, so that when I'm running from a knife-wielding lunatic, say, the buildings recur time and again:

I am in Sandy Hill racing through backyards and sailing over fences, slipping through hedges, in and around the university, over the Laurier Bridge, and then the Parliament buildings are before me, close and deserted, and on it goes, my killer as miraculously athletic as I am, still in pursuit as I run along Rideau back to Sandy Hill, back through the university, back over the bridge, back to Parliament, back . . .

And there you have it. Which city indeed. The city I know best is too intimate to share, not because I wouldn't share it with you, but because you must have rubbed against it at least as often as I have to understand that the Parliament buildings aren't the Parliament buildings so much as they are words in another language.

I mean, there are two strands of the city in my imagination. There's the city I walk in: the smell of summer on MacLaren as I pass Dundonald Park and hear the trees whisper . . . an inch of snow on the black railing beside the canal . . . inside the old Elgin Cinema down to the front row and take off my coat and say "Excuse me" as my elbow bumps the stranger beside me, "No problem, no problem" . . .

Then there's the city I negotiate in dreams and daydreams.

They aren't entirely distinct, of course. Ottawa feeds the city of my dreams, and the city of my dreams is a dimension of the city itself.

The War Memorial, for instance. The first time I remember seeing the monument, with its forbidding stone angel and dark soldiers moving through a white arch, I wasn't so much frightened as confused. Somewhere inside of me, the monument meant something more peculiar than Death or Heroism.

And then, years later, when something was broken in my life, I dreamed about the monument. I couldn't stop dreaming about it. The arch and the angel were white as milk, the soldiers like living shadows, whispering and grumbling as they tried to pull the cannon through. For some reason, the angel was angry, but angry as a shopkeeper might be at a difficult employee, and in anger it beat its wings, sending bright-red insects in every direction.

Whispering the cannon through the arch?

Red insects from stone feathers?

It doesn't matter what the dream meant, if it meant anything at all. The point is, it was vivid enough to stay with me for some time, and when next I saw the monument I didn't actually expect the angel to beat its wings, but the monument itself seemed as much a part of the city as a part of my self. It was a word in the shared language of my mind and my body.

I mean to say, Ottawa is a crucial messenger in the dialogue between my mind and my body. A short vocabulary of its language might look like this:

Body at:	Mind:
Bank Street:	boredom, beauty (Lansdowne), boredom (buses 1, 4, and 7)
Billings Bridge:	happiness (intellectual), despair (emotional)
Elgin Street:	desire, friendship (buses 14 and 5)
Major's Hill Park:	strange advances
War Memorial:	anxiety (death- or sex-related)
National Arts Centre:	friendship, quiet, hush
St. Laurent Blvd.:	desperation
Vanier:	anxiety *tout court* . . .

And so on through streets and buildings, alleys and lots, from the Market and Notre Dame to Blossom Park and Chinese food.

Of course, the words I've used (boredom, desire, etc.) are translated from a language that exists only in silence. And, to make matters worse, the language is constantly changing. The monument doesn't mean the same thing to me now as it did at one time. I can pass it without thinking of insects. It has gone from being a vivid line in a poem ("Ode to Ottawa") to a vivid sentence in a novel (*We So Seldom Look on Ottawa*), and when I die it will be a volume in an encyclopedia in which there's a vivid entry on red insects (*Encyclopedia Ottaviensis*, Thomas MacMillan, Editor).

I've been talking about Ottawa, but in a way I've also been talking about Henry Wing.

The idea of a secret language, for instance, was one of Henry's favorites. Encyclopedias were his obsession, and, in the matter of world and dream, I remember a day we sat together, eating sugar cake and drinking tea.

It was summer and I was eighteen when, out of the blue, Henry mentioned how much he wished his latest idea had come to him sooner.

— What idea?

— I'd like to write my oneirography.

— I'm sorry?

— Or is it my auto-oneirography? Whatever it should be called, I was thinking of writing my life story. Someone somewhere might learn from my steps, I thought. The problem is, my life has been so uneventful, an autobiography would bore me to tears, you know? How to make it interesting, that's the question. And it occurred to me that the most interesting things in my life have happened while I slept. And I thought: Wing, wouldn't it be wonderful to relive the life you and Kata have lived in dreams? And then I thought: Hold on a minute. Quite a number of people have dreamed of you over the years. If I could collect and cobble their dreams, that might be interesting. I bet I've lived a full life in the dreams of other people. If I could get them to tell me of dreams in which I've appeared, I could write my own life without the tedium of living it twice. That's what I mean by oneirography, Tom. An elegant solution, don't you think?

He sipped his tea and smiled.

I really did think it an elegant solution, though like any number of his ideas, it stayed with me longer than it did with him. Long after he'd abandoned his oneirography, the idea of it kept me amused.

(It amuses me still, yet I wonder if the difference between our lives and the lives we live in others isn't much less interesting than Henry supposed.)

It's difficult to say which of the two, Henry or Ottawa, I know best.

I met them on the same day, but I've been more intimate with the city since then. If it were suddenly turned into a human being, I'm certain I would recognize it. In fact, I sometimes think I am its embodiment. I am so thin and my eyesight so poor. I get along in both of its languages. My work is menial, but it has an official title: Senior Research Assistant, Lamarck Labs Inc.

On the other hand, despite my love for him, there are aspects of Henry Wing that still seem peculiar. If Henry were turned into a city, I don't think I'd recognize it at all. He himself admired third-century Alexandria and Renaissance Florence, cities of sensual learning. He tolerated Ottawa.

Though he never left the city, he managed to turn his little part of it into somewhere else.

Anyway, we had walked from Manotick.

Now that I think of it, my mother must have been in foul temper. She had a sniveling child, two suitcases to carry, and nowhere to go but to a man whom she had not intended to see.

She asked passersby for Cooper.

— Cooper?

— Cooper?

I assumed we were looking for someone named Cooper, though what we wanted was Cooper Street. And when we found 77 Cooper, it was a disappointment, a slightly grimy three-story house that might, at one time, have been fashionable but, in 1967, looked to be on its last legs.

(How wrong an impression can be. I am now writing these words at a desk on the second floor of 77, looking out the window toward Elgin. The house is doing well.)

We pushed the doorbell.

The door was opened by a dark old woman with red hair.

— Come in, come in, she said

as if she'd been expecting us.

The first floor was dimly lit, and the place smelled mildly of exotic cooking. The walls of the entranceway looked as if they hadn't been cleaned; they were whitish. But, as we passed a set of French doors, I caught a glimpse of a bright sitting room, with colorful carpet and wide windows. (My memory of the sitting room is in thrall to my love for it.)

My mother wasn't interested in the first floor, though. We made for the stairwell before us and climbed to the second.

Here too the walls appeared not quite clean, though they were papered a light blue. There was a sculpted plaster rose on the ceiling above the stairwell. From the center of the rose, a lightbulb in a frosted globe depended. This floor smelled faintly of lilac.

We turned sharply at the top of the stairs, my hand on the banister, and there, behind sliding-glass doors, was what looked to be a large living room. In the room, which Henry called a den, was a handful of laughing women sitting on high-backed chairs.

Actually, I don't remember how many women there were, and they seemed old, though they couldn't have been much older than Henry was then (forty). I remember red lips, an orchestra of jewelry: rings, bracelets, necklaces, earrings . . . And when my mother pushed the glass doors apart, the scent of lilac, and other flowers, was overwhelming.

It was an impressive display of femininity, though as I later learned, it's possible the women were actually men. Henry was neither transvestite nor homosexual himself, but he enjoyed the company of either, on the grounds that it kept him faithful to my mother, his beloved Kata.

As we entered, the laughter stopped. My mother said, as if she owned the room

— Excuse me, ladies, Mr. Wing and I need to speak.

It was then that I saw Henry Wing for the first time. He was standing in front of a blackboard at the far end of the den. He was wearing a gray, pinstriped suit with a white shirt, top button buttoned. I remember that suit and shirt, and I remember the numbers on a corner of the blackboard:

$$+40 \quad +4M$$
$$-40 \quad -4M$$

(The numbers were there forever.)

I have always thought Henry the most handsome man I've ever met. He was tall, slim, with a slightly unusual face: dark-brown eyes, high cheekbones, and ears a little too big. His hair was short, his fingers long and graceful. His skin was as dark as my mother's and he smelled of lemon soap, the bright-yellow bars of which were the only soap he kept about, so that, to this day, the bathrooms here hold a trace of him. For this I am, though I haven't always been, grateful.

He was handsome, but he wasn't quite aware of it. He always dressed well, with clean shirts and polished shoes, but the clothes were less impressive the closer one was. The pinstriped gray suit, for instance, was old and, at the elbows, the material was worn.

He carried himself as very few people do, seeming informal and attentive however straight he stood. From our first handshake to our last, I was at ease in his company.

My mother was in a state; disheveled, impatient, child in tow. The ladies rose from their armchairs and filed out of the room.

— Poor dear.

— We're just outside, Henry.

The perfume was sweet in their wake, and, when they had gone, Henry said

— Hooray, you routed the sirens

and then, looking at me

— And who's this?

— This is Thomas MacMillan, my mother answered. Thomas, would you leave us alone for a minute?

— Oh, but we haven't shaken hands, said Henry.

We shook hands, his kind face looking down at mine.

Once out of the room, the glass doors sliding shut behind me, I was in the company of the women (or of the men).

— Poor boy.

— Look how dirty he is.

— Doesn't your mother feed you, dear?

— What *does* the young woman want with Henry?

I was thankful for the attention.

I don't want to give you the wrong impression of Henry. I hope I haven't put too much emphasis on his eccentricities, what with the mention of oneirography and men dressed as women. If one can appreciate his passions, the most important of which were ideas and Katarina, he seems much less unusual.

In the matter of ideas, he was a connoisseur, as others are connoisseurs of butterflies, crickets, or scorpions. For the most part, he was a diligent amateur, keeping lists of unusual conceptions (see figure 3) and, as with most amateurs, the out-of-the-way gave him particular pleasure.

At times, he thought seriously of writing an encyclopedia, to be called *Wing's Abstractions: A Cyclopedia of Unusual Conceits*. He had twenty-six oversize, leather-bound "paste books" into which he glued articles, definitions, and original ideas. But, as with any encyclopedia, there were subtle problems to resolve before beginning:

1. How to order ideas?
   Alphabetically? By conceptual likeness? (Should Anthropomancy be included in an article on Hieromancy? Or should it be mentioned in a general article on strange uses of the human body?)
2. What to do with nameless ideas?
   What *do* you call the use of human skin for book binding? Or the various attempts to shorten the alphabet? And, names lacking, did he have the right to name ideas? (This wasn't a problem in the case of ideas he considered his

own—Archephilia, Partitionism, etc.—but to name a conception that belonged to someone else struck him as tiresome.)

3. What, precisely, constitutes "unusual"?
Here was a real problem. The idea that children are made when men grunt in the company of women, this is unusual but immature, a simple misconception. Should it be included? It might be mentioned in a general article on "Childish Misconceptions," but such an article could itself exhaust an encyclopedia. ("The sky is blue because the clouds aren't there," and so on . . .)
And then there were ideas that, though common, are still unusual: radio, for instance.
And, finally, there were ideas that are both common *and* usual, but which, on investigation, are as mysterious as the rarities: Dwelling, Time, Number, Cause and Effect. Why should they be excluded?

He never resolved any of these questions, and it was in this that Henry showed himself truly amateur. If he'd made *a* decision on any of them, as opposed to *the* decision, he might have finished the encyclopedia some time ago, immense though it was as an undertaking.

What he needed was single-mindedness, but that would have diminished his one real pleasure: the conception of unusual ideas. He spent hours, days, weeks leisurely meditating, trying to discover an idea that was original, potentially useful, and, to the best of his knowledge, as yet unnamed.

I don't know if it mattered how good or how appropriate his "new" ideas actually were. He took real pride in something like Archephilia, which is, to quote his handwritten entry in *Wing's*:

ARCHEPHILIA (from the Greek *arkhe* one, order + *philos* loving) (a: •kə•fíliə): 1. A love of order, manifest in the search for system (material or spiritual) in circumstances not obviously ordered. 2. In its metaphysical sense, *Archephilia* is the desire for dissolution in the oneness that precedes order. 3. (derogatory) The persistent search for order where none exists.

(Antonym: *Archephobia*: fear of order, resentment of God or anyone like him.)

Archephiles in History: Parmenides, Nicolas of Cusa, Giordano Bruno, John Donne, Isaac Newton.

○

diagram 1

Even by Henry's own modest rules, this isn't very convincing. It's more a description than an idea and, so, not entirely appropriate. Still, he took such pleasure in the sound of the word, he couldn't bring himself to exclude it from his work.

(It's sad that I should have opened *Wing's* to this particular entry. If Henry had loved order a little more, he'd have gone further. The disarray in which he left the encyclopedia, with illegible entries, blank pages, and nothing at all in volume eleven, is a memento of the qualities he lacked.)

It was only around my mother that he was, occasionally, absurd. I mean, Henry could be unbearably courtly, and when, from time to time, I saw that side of him, I understood why my mother wasn't always comfortable with him.

Now, in my admittedly personal understanding of Love, it's a time-based phenomenon. I mean, first love and infatuation are glandular matters, and once the glands are sore, there's still breakfast and bad humor, sharp toenails and flatulence, things it takes time to accept in oneself, let alone in another. That's not to say that I fall out of love at first fart, but, after the holiday of infatuation, I'm able to love with a clear head, accepting the things I find distasteful as part of the compact.

Though he didn't always behave as if he were infatuated, and though he is the only man I know of who truly loved my mother, there was a touch of the unbridled in Henry's feelings for her, as if every aspect of my mother were admirable.

Neither of them ever told me when or how they had met, but it was obvious they'd known each other for some time. From our first night in Henry's home, my mother grumbled about aspects of him I wouldn't discover until much later. And, though he had nothing but praise for her, he knew her qualities infinitely better than I did then.

(I suspected Henry was my father and, on our first night with him, I asked my mother if he were. And I remember her sitting on the edge of the big bed that had been prepared for me, in a bedroom that smelled of camphor.

— What a question, she answered.)

Despite his knowledge of my mother, Henry sometimes chose the most annoying ways to express his feelings. It was in this I thought him absurd. He would recite for me, but only in my mother's presence, the most sentimental poetry:

> *The long love that in my thought doth harbor,*
> *And in my heart doth keep his residence, . . .*

On the dining-room table, he put yellow carnations in a glass bowl filled with water. He would play recordings of madrigals after dinner. He bought colorful birds: a canary, turtledoves, a parrot.

He didn't do these things every day, you understand, nor all that often, now that I think of it, but it takes very little Thomas Wyatt and only a few madrigals to make me question a man's sense. And, it seems to me, if he'd loved her a little less, or less passionately, they might have been happier longer.

And yet . . .

And so . . .

Henry Wing, a black man with Chinese blood, handsome, tall, forty years old, in love with a woman eleven years younger, at work on an encyclopedia of limited appeal, living on Cooper Street in the city of my dreams, my father perhaps.

Considerate is the word for him, considerate and loving.

X

Now, once Henry dismissed the sirens, he led us downstairs to the dining room.

— Mrs. Williams, he called.

The old woman with red hair, whose slippers and rolled-down stockings I now noticed, shuffled amiably in.

— Yes, Mr. Wing?

— Mrs. Williams, I'd like you to meet Miss MacMillan and her son, Tom.

— Is a lovely boy you have there, miss.

— And I believe he's hungry, Henry said. What have we got that isn't frozen?

— Mr. Wing, you know I does never freeze anything. It have some okra and rice in the fridge.

— Would you like okra and rice? Henry asked.

I said

— Yes, please.

I could only have said "Yes, please" to okra once in my life, and I remember it still. The texture was repulsive. The rice, though, was a thing with pigeon peas and pieces of something salty that turned out to be pig tail. I ate every grain, rescuing some from under the okra.

— Thank you, Henry, my mother said when we'd finished.

— Did you like it, Tom?

— I didn't like the green, sir.

— Neither did your mother.

So, we never had okra again, though Mrs. Williams sometimes served callaloo, which is okra by other means. (Callaloo inevitably came with crab, however, and crab was the most exotic food I could imagine, and it was good.)

It's strange, now that I think of it, how easily I accepted as much of Mrs. Williams' cooking as I did. It was mostly Caribbean and, until I discovered Henry's Trinidadian descent, inexplicably foreign. Yet, I took to plantain and roti, dasheen and doubles as if I were born to them.

The food was appropriate to my new surroundings. Not that Henry's home was Caribbean. It wasn't, but it was more so than anything I'd known. My grandmother, after all, had swept Trinidad from her own life and surroundings. Here, in this household, buljol and sugar cake belonged.

At least, *I* felt that way. My mother almost certainly felt otherwise. Perhaps, when she was younger, my grandmother hadn't been quite so diligent in hiding her origins. In that case, the Caribbean aspect of Henry's home, Mrs. Williams in particular, would have been an unpleasant reminder of the place she'd fled.

I write all that without conviction, though. My mother was unkind to Mrs. Williams, but she may have had other reasons to dislike her. The thing is, I can't think of her behavior without remembering how little I understood it.

The household over which Mrs. Williams held tenuous sway was a reflection of its owner; in places extravagant, in places shabby.

The sitting room on the first floor was, of all the rooms, my

favorite. Its curtains were white. There were two scarlet tan-
agers, stuffed and mounted on the mantelpiece. There was a deep
red sofa, under whose cushions I could hide. And, for moments
of abandon, when I pushed the Persian rug aside, there was a
wide expanse of varnished wooden floor, clean and smooth
from sofa to dining room. In my stockinged feet, or standing on
my pajama bottoms, I could slide the length of it.

Almost as wonderful, and certainly more mysterious, were
the rooms across the entranceway: the library and the lab. The
laboratory was usually locked, except when Henry was using it,
but the library was open, unless Henry was reading in it. So, it
was the library I came to know first.

And a beautiful library it was. From floor to ceiling, the walls
were hidden by bookcases. In the bookcases, there were thousands of volumes, some crammed two rows to a shelf. Though
they were most of them leather-bound, there was the widest
variety imaginable: a collection of short stories by Sigrid Undset
and *The Marvellous Adventures of Nils Holgerson* were there
beside Averroës and Avicenna, the Marquis de Sade beside
St. Teresa of Ávila, Lane's *The Thousand and One Nights* with
Spinoza's *Ethics*, Gershom Scholem with Niels Bohr, *The Sara-
gossa Manuscript* with books on insects, mammals, birds, stars . . .

These books, and the thousands in the attic, in Henry's bedroom, in the basement, in the reading room on the second floor,
all of them fussed over and, in principle, dusted by Mrs. Williams,
were the sources for *Wing's Abstractions*. They were also, for
years, my main font of amusement, edification, and terror. I can't
describe the joy of discovering, for instance, J. B. S. Haldane's
Natural History of the Beetle, with its meticulous illustrations,
or the nightmares that followed a reading of *Lady into Fox*.

During our first months at Henry's, I was particularly diverted
by the library. It was spring, then it was summer. I had no

friends, and my mother and Henry engaged in hours of engagement. They did nothing but talk about the future. I couldn't spend five minutes in their company without getting bored.

So, I read.

Neither of them seemed at all concerned by what I read. I remember sitting in the library's armchair, reading with wonder, shame, and incomprehension *Les Bijoux indiscrets*, a novel about talking vaginas, when Henry came in, too quickly for me to hide the book.

— Ah . . . Diderot, he said

and went into the lab, locking the door behind him.

They were impressed that I liked books. In the midst of their own upheavals, they were probably relieved that I was so easily occupied.

Mrs. Williams was even more impressed. She would sometimes shuffle into the library, dust rag in hand, and watch me read, something she couldn't do herself.

— Uhm hmm, she'd say after a while, if he eyes last long as he fingers is a doctor for certain.

I pretended to ignore her, sinking deeper into the armchair, becoming even more serious, carefully turning the pages of my book, but I looked forward to her interruptions.

After the sitting room and the library, the room I liked best was my bedroom on the third floor. I might have preferred the kitchen and Mrs. Williams, were it not for the mice; not the mice themselves, which I loved, but the poor things cut in half in traps.

The bedroom wasn't entirely pleasant. It smelled of camphor, no matter how wide I opened the window. (To this day, I anticipate the smell, though there haven't been mothballs anywhere near it for some time.) The closet was a room in itself, wide enough to walk around in. That was fine in the day, but at night

I couldn't help thinking there was someone in it, and it kept me awake, listening.

My bed, though, my bed with its clean sheets, was a white lake. It was large enough for four or five of me and it was safe.

In our years with Henry, my mother came in to wish me good night, every evening. At first, it was an unexpected intimacy. She'd sit by the side of the bed and we would talk about the day, like confidants.

— I don't know how much longer we can stay here.

— Why not?

— Henry's wearing me down. It's too much being here.

— Where're we going to go?

— I don't know, but as soon as I find work, we'll find a place of our own. Is that okay?

— I guess so.

— And what about your day? What did you do?

— Well . . . I read in the library . . .

. . . I was sick . . .

. . . I couldn't . . .

. . . I didn't . . .

. . . I did . . .

I don't remember my answers as well as I do some of hers. Once or twice a week, I tried to impress her with some scrap of learning I'd taken in.

— Did you know there were 250,000 species of beetles?

— No, I didn't.

— And fireflies are . . .

Most often, though, I couldn't think of anything to say. Nothing ever happened to me. I did nothing worth talking about. So we would kiss good night, my mother turning off the light as she left, my room slowly flooding with moonlight and with such light as ran beneath the door.

When we'd gotten to know each other, when he'd begun to teach me the elements, Henry too would wish me good night, sometimes with my mother, sometimes after her.

— Good night, Tom.

— Good night, Mr. Wing.

It was "Mr. Wing" for a year before it was "Henry."

Henry seemed to have almost equal affection for Mrs. Williams and my mother.

As soon as I discovered how kind she was, I'd sit in the kitchen as Mrs. Williams made lunch or supper. I helped her clean up, or bent down for her when her back was bad and she couldn't stoop for the pots and pans. I did all this whenever I was tired of reading, or tired of hiding; hiding for its own sake, I mean, since there was no one to come looking for me.

There was usually something we could do together, but when there wasn't, I sat and listened to her, enchanted by the way she spoke. She was a generous teller of tales; one story flowed leisurely into the next.[8]

---

[8] The only one I still remember was about "No Nose" Brackley. The story was that No Nose, who had no nose and was one of the ugliest men in Trinidad, still managed to attract women once in a while, though he wasn't bright, and he wasn't wealthy, and he was "low class" . . .

—. . . An' it hav' a woman was drinkin' in Pepper Pot wit' No Nose, an' dis same woman decide she goin' an' take No Nose Brackley home for company, but she don' wan' to be seen wit' he at all, because she livin' wit' a family quite up in St. Clair where it high class. An' she say how he musn' touch anyt'ing, an' stay away from de windows, because she 'fraid someone goin' an see No Nose in de people home. Why de woman want dis nasty man, I don't know. It have some women basodi, yuh heah. An' he mus' be say "Doo doo" an' tell she

139

It was in this kitchen I first smelled cumin or bit into a pod of cardamom or, fearlessly, chewed a small piece of Scotch bonnet. Here also, I sliced ginger for a ginger beer so strong it was like drinking lye, and first smelled sorrel boiling down to what was my favorite drink. (I haven't had it or Mauby for years. I never learned to make them, and when Mrs. Williams left, Henry didn't have the heart to make them himself.)

Whenever he was waiting for a tincture of this to react with a tincture of that, Henry sat at the kitchen table with me. He quietly listened to Mrs. Williams's voice, opening jars of chutney, for the smell of them, and helping me roll tamarind pulp in sugar. Slight entertainment for a grown man, I thought, but he spent so much time in the kitchen, I understood he had real affection for Mrs. Williams.

Mrs. Williams had run of the entire house. She had keys to the most private rooms: the laboratory and Henry's bedroom.

It's true she took her time with the cleaning, and parts of the house always looked shabby, but dusting wasn't the work to which she was best suited; and, really, there was no one to criticize her. Henry was happy with her, my mother was often out looking for work, and I liked her too much to complain.

If Mrs. Williams had a failing, it was in her attitude to my

"don' worry," because he spend de night by she . . . Nex' mornin' de poor woman wake up, an what she see? No Nose Brackley on she balcony. De man in he underwear, an he callin' de neighbors

— Mornin', neighbors. Is nice weader we havin'. Mornin', madame. How de chil'ren?

De woman so shame, she have to move from St. Clair quite to San Fernando . . .

(If I made Mrs. Williams tell this one over and over, it was not because I understood it, but because I loved the way she imitated No Nose as he stood on the balcony.)

mother. She was a little spiteful. She couldn't accept that my mother, however unwittingly, had usurped some of her ground and most of her authority. There was no doubt where Henry stood in the matter, either. I remember hearing Mrs. Williams say
— But Miss MacMillan wash she face wit' Brasso? How she could tell me I musn't use pepper in a peas and rice?
— I know you're upset, Hilda, but it hurts me to hear you speak that way. If Kata doesn't want pepper, you should throw the peppers out.
Henry wasn't angry, but I could see Mrs. Williams was offended. Perhaps she'd only meant to test the waters, to see how far the currents had changed, and Henry had shown her, without hesitation, the new boundary of her existence. Everywhere her authority was circumscribed by my mother's, even here in the center of her influence, the kitchen.
— As you wish, Mr. Wing. I was only askin'. . .
I thought of Mrs. Williams as ancient, but she couldn't have been much more than sixty. Her face was dark and smooth, her eyes a soft brown, and some of her teeth were, intriguingly, false. Knowing how fascinating I found them, she sometimes left her teeth in a glass of salty water on the kitchen table. Her hair was red from henna, and she often wore a bright-yellow kerchief to keep it in place.
When Henry told her to throw the peppers out, her face crinkled.
— I was only askin'. . .
And so, she threw a small basket of red and yellow Scotch bonnets out into the garden.
Although that moment was the first in which I realized Mrs. Williams was at daggers drawn with my mother, theirs was a long skirmish that took place just outside my ken, and its end came much later.

By pure coincidence, I associate Mrs. Williams's defeat with the first visits I was allowed to Henry's small lab.

We'd been living on Cooper for some time.

I was in grade seven at Elgin, a school with a stone exterior and narrow halls. The classrooms smelled of chalk dust and the desks were cold in the morning. I remember little else about it.

It was my second year at the school. I was at ease at Henry's, though it still felt as if my mother and I were on the verge of leaving.

Not that my mother and Henry weren't getting along; they were. Each had evolved a routine that depended on the other, and my mother relaxed in his company. For his part, Henry did his best to stay out of her way. He knew that his feelings, however subtly expressed, made her a little nervous.

You know, God keep their souls, they were both of them strange, especially that year. A simple movement of the hand or head carried so much meaning, I couldn't always tell what they felt for each other from moment to moment.

At night, my mother was as likely to say

— I think we should be moving

as

— Would you mind if we stayed?

When she found work at Revenue Canada, we actually spent time, on weekends, looking for places to rent.

Yet, despite my mother's ambivalence, Henry and I grew very close.

When he learned of my first lessons in chemistry, he was pleased.

— Well, he asked, what did they tell you about chemistry?

We had learned about osmosis and chlorophyll and photosynthesis. Mr. Parker, our science teacher, drew green plants, a yellow sun, white clouds, and a blue sky in colored chalk on the blackboard.

— Osmosis *and* photosynthesis? Henry asked.

— Yes, both of them.

— Was it interesting?

— Yes. The plants turn carbon dioxide and water into . . .

We were in the library, and I was holding the oversize book on flowers that had stimulated our conversation. It was after school, but an hour at least before my mother would be home.

— If you have a few minutes, Tom, I'd love to show you something.

Taking the key from his pants pocket, Henry unlocked the door to the lab and led me in.

It wasn't what I expected, but it was far from disappointing. To begin with, it was spotless. The white linoleum floor, the white walls, the white ceiling. Everything was immaculate. There was one window. It looked out onto the house next door and, beneath the window, there was a deep aluminum sink with gleaming faucet and taps.

In the center of the room was a long, narrow, and solid wooden table on which there were beakers, glass tubes, and what looked to be black rubber stoppers.

Against the wall were metal shelves crowded with jars and more beakers, glass containers of every shape filled with a bewildering variety of powders, liquids, and solids. And, hanging like a family portrait beside one of the shelves, there was an elegant, three-dimensional periodic table: a shallow, white plastic grid in a wooden frame. In every square of the grid, there was a sample or representation of an element, along with its name, atomic number, atomic symbol, and atomic weight.

Henry took the periodic table down from the wall and put it in my hands.

— Tom, this is the most important thing in the lab. I'd like you to keep it for a while. If you learn the names and numbers of all the elements, we'll shake some of them up together. Would you like that?

— Very much, I said.

The idea of experiments fascinated me, as it would any eleven-year-old. Just the thought of mixing chemicals in vials, of making nitroglycerine, of watching liquids unexpectedly change color and bubble over. It was more exciting than anything I could think of.

It took me little more than a week to memorize the symbols, names, and numbers. To this day, I can look at things, at a silver bracelet, say, and think "47, Ag, 107.868, *Argentum,*" as if the periodic table were before me.

I wasn't immediately allowed back into the inner sanctum, though. Days after I swore I'd memorized them, Henry quizzed me on symbols or numbers.

— Tom, I can't remember which element is 70, can you?

— Tom, what was the symbol for iron, again?

— Tom, iridium's 42, isn't it?

Only when he was satisfied I'd mastered the table did Henry set aside a day and a time for us to make sodium chloride.

— Sodium chloride?

— Salt.

Salt? What a disappointment. Of all the things we could create, salt was the least interesting.

— Okay, I said.

— You don't want to make salt?

— I guess so.

— It's humble, but it's a beautiful compound. Well, we *could* start with something a little more appealing. How would you like to make gold, for instance?

— Gold? Can we make gold?

— Of course, Henry answered.

He smiled and put his arm around my shoulders.

— We'll do it the old way, he said.

The "old way," as it turned out, was to transform a baser element into gold through a series of encounters with the elixir. Transmutation is what it was called, every element having, in principle, the potential to become gold, the highest element.

Henry spoke of this as if there were nothing less mysterious. To help me understand the process, he added that the elixir, or grand magistery, worked in the most banal way. It taught the elements beneath gold (from hydrogen to platinum) of their potential, and reminded those above it (from mercury on up) of their highest moment.

It all made perfect sense to me.

— Can I see the grand magistery? I asked.

— Actually, Tom, you're going to get the elixir for me. There are so many thieves in this city, I keep it where no one would look.

That was certainly true. We went out to the backyard.

When we reached the garden, Henry looked back at the house and said, quietly

— Do you see that opening under the porch?

— Yes.

— I want you to crawl under there and go toward the back door. Right under the door there's a paper bag. In the paper bag there's a stone. Bring it to me, please.

He spoke so solemnly, I was thrilled to crawl under the porch. There were spiderwebs everywhere, and anthills. It must also have been gloomy and dark, but I didn't really notice. There, exactly where Henry said it would be, was the paper bag and, inside, there was a rock. You couldn't call it anything else. I held it in the palm of my hand to feel its power, and I did feel it; though, by such light as came through the slats of the porch, I could see it was a rock.

— Wonderful, Henry said as I handed him the paper bag. Now go and wash. We'll carry on tomorrow.

— Tomorrow?

— Yes, Tom. Don't you trust me?

— But . . .

It wasn't a matter of trust. I trusted him less than I'd trusted my mother when she asked me to steal, but I believed Henry, believed the magistery was mysterious and powerful. Tomorrow?

— But . . .

— Go and wash, Tom. And don't worry.

That night, I was awake for hours trying to picture the workings of the magistery. I understood it could remind mercury of its place, but what about glass? If we could turn glass to gold, I would spend my days collecting bottles, making real money from them, instead of the pennies I gathered for comic books.

And what would I do with the money, exactly?

Naturally, I had desires typical of an eleven-year-old. I wanted bicycles (Schwinn), swimming pools, and go-carts. I wanted an immense home on endless grounds. I wanted animals, running shoes, a ham radio . . . and all of this, now within reach, was so exciting I had trouble lying still.

The rooms of my dream house were large and white, with windows looking onto streams and meadows. The books I wanted were dark, leather-bound, and brightly illustrated. One of them in particular, which I almost certainly dreamed, though I don't remember sleeping, was so vividly engraved that when I opened it to a drawing of spiders, spiders (minute, precise, and ink black) scuttled from the pages.

That was the kind of thing I thought gold could give.

The following morning, I was as awake as if I'd slept soundly. I couldn't wait for the end of breakfast. I couldn't wait for my mother to leave, for Henry to call me to the lab. Everything happened slowly. Breakfast seemed endless, my mother couldn't leave fast enough, and Henry was so upset about the raccoons that had pitted his garden, his only thought was how best to keep them from his property. He didn't seem at all interested in gold.

— Aren't we going to the lab today? I asked.

— I'm sorry, Tom. Of course we are.

And, finally, though his thoughts were elsewhere, Henry took me to the lab.

I remember exactly how the lab looked on this morning: magical. It was clear Henry hadn't forgotten our task at all. On the usually uncluttered table, there was a skyline of beakers, stoppers, pipettes, alembics, and Bunsen burners. It is one of the few times in my life that the outside world has equalled my imagination of it. I wouldn't have added a beaker or subtracted a tube.

— So, Tom, what do you see?

I described everything around me.

— That's excellent, Henry said.

He pointed to the second and third alembics in a row of four.

— Now this is where the real change happens. Keep your eyes on these two.

In the second alembic there was a black stone in clear fluid; in the third, a white stone in what appeared to be the same liquid, too thick to be water, too thin to be mercury, though the stones, smooth and round as cat's-eye marbles, seemed almost to float in it.

— Watch carefully, Tom.

Henry took the rock I'd recovered from under the porch and put it in the final beaker in the series, a beaker filled with . . . ?

— Water.

In which, to my surprise, the rock floated.

— What shall we turn to gold? Henry asked.

— I don't know.

— All right, why don't we use what's in my pocket?

— Okay.

Henry lit the Bunsen burners beneath the alembics, precisely adjusted each of their flames, and then brought a crumpled paper bag from his pocket. It was filled with what looked suspiciously like dirt, but he carefully and ceremoniously tapped the contents into the first of the alembics.

— What is it? I asked.

— Raccoon manure, he said.

As it came to a boil, the liquid in the first alembic turned brown and then made its way through a pipette to the second alembic. Here, it was as if the black stone were ink. The liquid darkened and then made its way to the third alembic, where, miraculously, it whitened and foamed into the final alembic, in which the magistery floated.

When the process was finished, there being no more manure in the first three alembics, Henry carefully closed off the burners. We waited until things cooled a little, and then he poured the white liquid, and the magistery itself, onto a fine cheesecloth stretched over a shallow pan. Then he gently flooded the cloth with hot water.

I can't describe the excitement I felt as a tidy layer of gold emerged from the white dross. I looked up at Henry's face and saw that he was staring at me. He smiled as if to say: Yes, it's wonderful.

— Can we do it again? I asked.

— We could change manure to gold as often as you like, Tom, but think how disappointing that would be.

It wouldn't have been disappointing to me at all, but I nodded sagely, as if I understood, and watched as he slowly dismantled the city of alembics.

— Can I keep it? I asked, pointing to the gold.

— Of course, Tom, but where are you going to put it? You can't keep the dust in your pocket, you know.

We put the dust in a white envelope addressed to "Mr. Henry Wing, esq." I folded the envelope in half, and then again in half, so that it fit nicely at the bottom of my pants pocket. (I have them still, the envelope and the last of the gold dust. Although the paper has darkened, and the address is legible only if you know where to look, it is the envelope that means most to me now.)

— Thank you, Henry, I said.

— Think nothing of it, he answered. Close the door on the way out, will you, Tom?

He was already distracted by whatever it was that came next.

I understand Mrs. Williams disliked my mother, but I don't understand how she could so thoroughly have underestimated the force of Katarina's personality. I had misjudged my mother, it's true, taking her soft voice and calm exterior for a peaceful mind and stable outlook, but I was a child. Mrs. Williams should have known better.

Sometime after Henry's work with the magistery, the mood in our home soured.

It was either late fall or early winter. Henry and I had already made our excursion to the jeweler's, to exchange some of my gold for dollars. The jeweler, a gray-haired man with shaky hands, looked down at me with an attentiveness I found embarrassing and held out an impossible clump of money; seventy-nine dollars in small bills, the most money I had ever seen and, in some ways, the most money I will ever see. As we left the shop, the streets were white with snow.

It wasn't open warfare between my mother and Mrs. Williams; though, considering how goldstruck I was, it must have been a bitter struggle for me to notice their conflict at all. I mean, I was so preoccupied I could barely pay attention at school and, though I'd agreed to keep it secret, I was dying to tell my friends about Henry's transformation of raccoon manure; my friends being Rachel and Mickie Jordan, Todd Roberts, and Howie Redhill.

Despite my mother's occasional, spiteful mention of Mrs. Williams, I assumed their respective places were clear. Henry had come so squarely down on my mother's side in the altercation over Scotch bonnets, I don't see how Mrs. Williams could have been confused.

It seems strange to me, now, that she should have bothered to skirmish at all. My mother was uncomfortable in the role of "Mistress Wing." If Mrs. Williams had waited patiently, meekly, she would certainly have returned to power, and the MacMillans' time at Henry Wing's might have been an interregnum only.

But something in her would not accept my mother.

Perhaps Mrs. Williams could be kind, but not meek; considerate, but not self-effacing; good-humored, but not hypocritical.

I'm speculating on things I know nothing about. It's equally possible Mrs. Williams was purely self-interested, that Henry was a benefactor she refused to share, or even that, in her own way, she was in love with Henry.

What I noticed, and then only occasionally, were little signs of conflict and things that were ambiguous until after Mrs. Williams's defeat:

- her hands shook when she set a plate before my mother
- she grew rigid in my mother's presence
- her voice was toneless when she spoke to my mother
- she began to call me an "unfortunate" child and took up my education, teaching me old and peculiar songs like "Caroline" and "Gold Bond soap to wash your punkalunks."

And how did my mother respond?

- she was, at times, ostentatiously agreeable
- at night, there were, occasionally, unkind words about Mrs. Williams: "that old . . . ," "that wrinkled . . . ," "that nasty . . ."

And Henry?

- he seemed even less observant than I, noticing neither Mrs. Williams's insubordination nor Katarina's reactions.

So, the end of Mrs. Williams's reign came in winter, some time after I'd exchanged my palmful of dust for money.

There had been an awkward exchange between my mother and Mrs. Williams. My mother casually mentioned that she found it eccentric to wear slippers around the house.

Mrs. Williams, who wore slippers, took offense. She stiffened, and walked out of the dining room without a word, as though nobly bearing an injury. From that day on, she wore nothing but shoes, without socks, the same shoes: black with low heels; shoes that, unfortunately, bore a strong resemblance to a pair my mother owned.

And one night, a week or so after her remark about slippers, as she wished me good night, my mother finally let it out.

— I can't stand that woman, she said.

— Who?

— She's ruining us.

— Who?

— Mrs. Williams. I don't know why Henry keeps her around.

— Mrs. Williams?

I could tell my mother was upset. Though her voice was soft, she kept a hand on my shoulder as she spoke.

— Haven't you noticed her shoes?

— Her shoes?

— She took my shoes.

— She borrowed them?

— She took them.

It wasn't clear to me why Mrs. Williams would take my mother's shoes, and, given what happened in Alliston (or Bradford), I wasn't inclined to take my mother's word for it, but she did something I didn't expect. My mother asked me to say I'd seen Mrs. Williams take her shoes.

— But I didn't see her take your shoes, I said.

— You didn't see anything with your eyes, my mother answered, but that's not important.

How elegant.

I've always been susceptible to fine thinking and, though my mother didn't always stoop to it, her thinking was particularly fine when she wished it. So what if I hadn't "seen with my eyes"? This wasn't about shoes. It wasn't about theft, and it wasn't about guilt. Mrs. Williams had so poisoned the small world we shared, it wasn't possible to go on. She would have to leave, or we would, and if it took a little subterfuge to oust the woman, what of it?

I had come to adore Mrs. Williams, but I sided with my mother. This subterfuge was a new intimacy between us.

The following evening, we sat at our places around the table, Henry, my mother, and I. Mrs. Williams had prepared an elaborate meal, and the food itself seemed an act of defiance, with everything spicy enough to make your lips tingle.

I vividly remember Mrs. Williams from these last moments: impassive, silent, a little frail, shuffling, head bowed, shoes clacking noisily on the floor. Everything about her was end-of-the-day weary, and yet she kept up her small defiance, a coldness toward my mother, perhaps imagining that, after all, she would outlast her, that this meal was one less she would have to prepare for "Miss MacMillan."

Once we'd eaten, my mother called Mrs. Williams back to the dining room and, softly, said

— Henry, Thomas has something to tell us.

The three of them looked to me, and I looked back, deeply interested in the proceedings, not nervous at all, curious about the effect my words would have.

— Mrs. Williams stole my mother's shoes, I said.

It was thrilling to say it.

— What's that? Henry asked.

— Mrs. Williams stole my mother's shoes.

Henry stared at me, as if he'd missed something crucial.

— I steal he mother shoes? Mrs. Williams asked.

She looked at me as if I'd spoken in a foreign language.

— She's wearing them now, my mother answered (softly).

— It ain' true, said Mrs. Williams (coldly).

How absurd this was. Mrs. Williams would have to have been addle-brained to steal my mother's shoes and parade around in them. And yet . . . perhaps Mrs. Williams imagined my mother would not notice the loss or, noticing, that she would be too polite to say anything. For Henry's sake, I leave as much room as I can for Mrs. Williams's guilt, though I think he knew how ridiculous all of this actually was.

Once I'd said what I had to say, the adults turned away from me.

— It ain' true, Mrs. Williams repeated.

A silence followed, a silence that stretches and contracts in my memory, moments during which Mrs. Williams held herself as upright as she was able, her red hair tucked behind her ears.

Absurd though the accusation was, my mother didn't offer a syllable in its defense. She calmly stared at Mrs. Williams, until Henry said

— I'm very sorry, Hilda . . . I'm afraid you'll have to leave us.

— But, Mr. Wing, dese shoes kyar fit Miss MacMillan.

A crucial point and, to drive it home, she stepped out of her shoes, clumsily, leaning forward on the table to push one off with the other.

No one looked at the shoes.

— I'm very sorry, Henry repeated, but you'll have to leave us.

Another strained silence, with Henry looking down at his plate, and my mother staring at the old woman until, with all the dignity she could manage, Mrs. Williams said

— Is I sorry for you, Henry.

In my lifetime I have watched thousands and thousands of people leaving rooms. It is never the same. Though it is you who are left behind, there are some people one leaves with, and some one abandons without moving. Mrs. Williams was wearing a white sweater. (Her dress was calf-length, light blue, and her back looked so narrow.) At the time, her exit struck me as neither sad nor pathetic. It was the logical conclusion to something or other, but although I have sometimes imagined *I* abandoned Mrs. Williams, a part of me walked out with her.

— Thank you, my mother said as Mrs. Williams left.

— You're welcome, Kata, Henry answered.

Just like that.

And yet . . .

The incident thrives in my subconscious, always supposing I have one, as I'm convinced it thrived in Henry's.

It's a difficult thriving to delineate. If I feel troubled by Mrs. Williams's departure, it has less to do with my having lied than with the way I lied. It must have been clear to everyone that my words were a pretext, proof that I took my mother's side in this campaign. I was only a catalyst. You couldn't even call it lying, really. It was more like a thoughtless devotion.

Nor was I altogether disappointed by the results. The three of us, Henry, my mother, and I, did grow closer, however briefly, once Mrs. Williams was out of the picture.

No, the thing that troubles me is how easy, how fascinating it was to lie, how completely poor Mrs. Williams was obliterated.

Henry's feelings on the matter are even more difficult to describe. He couldn't have sided with Mrs. Williams any more than I, but *he* must have known we'd been unfaithful. I imagine he was as disappointed in me as he was in himself, and though it wasn't in him to punish me, the way he closed the door on gold-making seems as much a rebuke as it was a lesson.

Weeks after Mrs. Williams's defeat, I was still flush with the money I'd made from our gold. I bought comics (*Spiderman*, *Iron Man*, *Doctor Strange*), Converse All Stars, a shortwave radio. I spent happily, believing there would be no end to fortune. Seventy-nine dollars was so much money, it took me two months to exhaust.

At the end of that exhilarating time, I decided I needed a new coat, something less bulky than the one I had, and blue instead of green. I was so pleased with my decision to spend practically, I resolved to be even more practical in the future. That is, it finally occurred to me I could also buy things for others, for my mother and for Henry, though that would mean making even more gold so I could have as much for myself.

It was with a feeling of largesse, of generosity, that I asked Henry if we could make more gold.

— What would you like, Tom?

I explained to him, in great detail, how important it was for me to have more money, how sorry I was not to have discovered my generosity sooner, but, now that I had, he and my mother would be its chief beneficiaries. There were so many things I could do for them.

— How much do you need, Tom?

And, supposing it to be a simple matter of using three times as much raccoon manure, I asked for three times as much money: two hundred and thirty-seven dollars.

Without blinking, as if it were the most natural thing in the world to give a twelve-year-old hundreds of dollars, Henry reached into the inner pocket of his suit coat and extracted five twenty-dollar bills.

— I don't have that much just now, he said. Here's a hundred. I'll give you the rest this evening.

He hasn't understood at all, I thought. I didn't want his money. That would have been wrong. I wanted to make more

gold—which we could do any time we wanted, couldn't we?—
and though the process was a little more convoluted, I would
prefer, Henry, to transmute a little raccoon manure.

— Couldn't we?

— Are you sure? Henry asked.

— Yes, please.

— As you like, Tom. You know where to find the magistery.

Indeed I did, and though it wasn't yet spring, and the ground
was wet, I crawled beneath the porch as if it were the sunniest
place on earth, proud that Henry now trusted me to recover the
stone on my own, proud again of my newfound maturity. I had
in mind a leather wallet for Henry and fur-lined gloves for my
mother.

Henry called me into the laboratory later the same day.

I was even more excited this time, though I was a little less
interested in the mechanism of transformation. The beautiful
skyline of beakers, alembics, and burners was set up as it had
been, a Pyrex version of ultima Thule, but I was anxious to
exchange our gold for money, right away this time, same day,
please and thank you.

— It's too wet for manure, Henry said. What shall we use?

— Anything, I said.

— How about cotton then, Tom?

— That's a good idea, Henry.

When everything was ready, when the liquids were properly
perturbed and the magistery floated gracefully, Henry took a
handful of cotton wool from a drawer and, with black scissors,
cut it into dust over the first beaker.

— Will that make three times as much? I asked.

— It should.

And when the particles of cotton had made their way to the
magistery, they were transformed and, once the water washed

over the white muck, there really did appear to be three times as much gold.

— Henry? Do you think we could go to the jeweler's now?

— Of course, Tom, of course.

We went to W. A. Irwin Jewellery on Bank, because it was closest. Henry had given me a clean handkerchief, in the center of which we'd let the gold fall. The ends of the kerchief were tied with string. I took it carefully from my pocket and set it on Mr. Irwin's glass countertop.

— How much can you give us for this? Henry asked the jeweler.

— What is it?

— Gold.

— How many carats?

— Twenty-four.

— Hmmm . . .

The jeweler, a tall, bearded man with dark-rimmed glasses, rubbed some of the dust into a clump.

— There isn't much, he said, pouring the dust into the vessel of a delicate scale. Less than a quarter . . . It isn't much use to me, really . . . Ten? I suppose I could use it for small work, links and such . . . Ten, if you throw in the handkerchief.

— Thank you, Henry said.

I was confused and disappointed. As soon as we left the shop, I asked why he'd accepted only ten dollars for so much gold.

— It wasn't worth more, he said.

— But it was three times as much as last time!

— And what does that tell you, Tom?

For the life of me, I couldn't understand.

— Mr. Irwin must have cheated us.

— Not at all.

— But . . .

We walked slowly along Bank, past Cooper, on toward Somerset, past gray buildings that are even more gray in my memory. At Somerset, we turned west, away from home.

— What would happen if we could make as much gold as we wanted? Henry asked.

I looked up at him.

— We could buy anything we wanted, I answered.

— Not for long, Tom.

At Bronson we turned back, and then walked north on Lyon, east on Cooper.

— There's no such thing as a magistery, he said.

On the bottom of each of the alembics, there had been a thin layer of wax in which motes of gold were embedded.

— But . . .

He had paid the first jeweler to buy our bit of gold.

What a pointless and cruel hoax, I thought. It took me some time to forgive him this betrayal, longer still to understand it, but Henry himself took no pleasure in my humiliation.

As we went into 77 Cooper, he said

— You should have taken the money, if that's what you wanted.

My thoughts exactly, at the time, though not of late.

XI

—

I have been writing this for months now.

I've been writing for four months, and I'm surprised at how much, and how little, of myself has made it to these pages; how much, though I've been writing of others, yet how few of my own details there are. I mean:

What was I like?

What clothes did I wear?

What was the sound of my voice?

Still, the pleasure I take in writing, if you can call it pleasure, is the pleasure of being with others. So long as I am with Mother, with Henry, the details of my own life seem important.

Besides, at the time of which I'm writing, my life *was* their life. And, when Mrs. Williams left, I was even more fascinated by the two of them.

Did they love each other?

I've written what I know of my mother's early life, but little of that helped me understand if she loved Henry. He was not like Mr. Mataf, after all.

Did they touch?

I was uneasy about their sexual life. I don't like to imagine either of them naked, but they were both such sensual people, they couldn't have lived together without touching, and, without really knowing, I knew that they touched.

But how?

Their sensualities were expressed in different ways. Outwardly, at least, my mother was not as "refined" as Henry. I don't imagine she needed thirteenth-century Persian manuscripts, candlelight, or Purcell's *Dido and Aeneas* to inspire her.

Henry, on the other hand . . .

When she chose him for refuge, my mother was in distress. We were on our way to Montreal and life with Mr. Mataf. So, our long walk to Ottawa was certainly unplanned.

And yet, she entered Henry's home with authority, knowing its layout, knowing where to find him, confident Henry would interrupt whatever he was doing to speak with her. She must also have known that Henry would take both of us in without protest. I can't imagine her imposing otherwise.

These are crucial things to know about another person.

Perhaps, sometime in the distant past, Henry had said, "Kata, if you're ever in trouble, please let me help." He must have impressed her with his sincerity, must have convinced her that "Let me help" meant let me help.

In that distant past, something essential must have been exchanged (confidence, trust, warm words . . .) and the twenty-nine-year-old Katarina, abandoned in Manotick, remembering their intimacy, made her way to Mr. Wing, his home.

(I'm putting my own face on things, with this business of confidence and warm words. Isn't it possible that the two met briefly, that Henry fell in love and offered whatever he could to win her over? My mother, recognizing her advantage and sensing she had the wherewithal to keep him to his word, familiarized herself with his home and left with a potent weapon: his infatuation.

And this she used when she found herself in trouble.

This is a darker version of Katarina's state of mind, but if I've given the impression it was possible for my mother to behave this way, I've misled you, and I think I can rule out this parenthetical version of events before the end of my parenthesis.

To begin with, Henry was not blind. My mother couldn't have convinced him it was possible for her to love unless it really were possible.

And then, my mother hated weakness, in herself, in me, in Henry. It would have repulsed her to live with a man who

a) couldn't tell affection from manipulation
b) allowed himself to be so obviously used.

And, finally, though she was certainly manipulative, my mother was a talented and unpredictable manipulator, an artist who enjoyed her craft. What talent would it have taken to manipulate Henry if he were weak?

These days, when I consider her life, or those pieces of it I know, I think of my mother as a woman who learned early to fend for herself in a hostile environment: Petrolia. She broke herself in pieces, the better to hide the essential. She was one thing to her mother, another to her friends, and still another to strangers. She was a romantic ideal to Henry, and any number of things to me.

Aside from an accidental pregnancy—myself, though I don't rule out the possibility I was a child of love—she made her way in the world without often losing hold of herself, though she sometimes tried desperately to lose it—in love, for instance.

All of this makes the simple duping of Henry unthinkable.

It wouldn't have met her needs. From the beginning, there must have been some affection between them.

Quod erat demonstrandum. End parenthesis.)

Of course, my mother's age may also have played a part in her decision to stay with Henry. Now that I am on the other side of twenty-nine, I understand she was at that point in life when the future seems to hold fewer occasions for change. Putting herself in the home of a man who loved her may have been her way of courting change.

She certainly chose an interesting environment for it.

Henry's home, his person, his behavior . . . all of these were unusual.

Why would a twentieth-century man, Trinidadian at that, choose to live in a Victorian setting, with a gentleman's lab, old-fashioned books, and courtly attitudes that would have marked him as "stuffy" centuries ago?

I have sometimes thought Henry misguided or eccentric. I've thought him laughable or bizarre, all depending on my distances from him: temporal, physical, or psychological. Lately, though, I see in him another version of my grandmother.

They had different personalities, of course, but my grandmother's fanatic attachment to Lampman and Dickens, her disapproval of anything that might link her to Trinidad . . . these things had their echo in Henry.

He was born in 1927, in Port of Spain. His parents died when he was young and, after their deaths, Henry was passed from relation to relation like a chair, until, in 1934, he was sent to live with the "third cousin of a second cousin of a first cousin" who had recently moved to Canada, of all places, and who needed, truth be told, inexpensive help for a corner shop he owned in Sandy Hill.

Henry's distant cousin, a white-haired ogre named Maurice

Wing, was bitterly disappointed to discover a reed-thin seven-year-old instead of the able-bodied youth he'd been promised, but he put Henry to work nonetheless: sweeping up, tending the register, putting things on shelves, taking them off.

Reading was the one pleasure he was consistently allowed, on the grounds that it made him a more trustworthy cashier. So, the young Henry was an obsessive reader, poring over the books Mr. Wing sold in his shop, or books borrowed from the library, or books rescued from trash bins in the neighborhood, books abandoned by university students.

Henry's childhood was far from idyllic. He had no friends, no time for friends, and no company, save the baleful presence of Maurice Wing. He wasn't often beaten, he was fed, and, in time, he came to respect Mr. Wing enough to take his name, but . . .

When the man died and Henry inherited the shop at Templeton and Russell, he sold it as quickly as he could and moved on.

That handful of sentences holds most of the facts I have ever known about Henry's early life. I don't even remember his real name. In all the years I knew him, I was never young enough to have been told more, by way of bedtime stories, say, nor yet mature enough to take genuine interest in his life.

You'd think Henry would hold on to the Trinidad of his early happiness, but I suppose any version of the island brought with it the painful memory of abandonment. Canada, his new home, must have seemed vague and impersonal, if only because what he knew best was the inside of a small shop in Sandy Hill, not much to go on and too little to love. And so, as I see it, he took such parts of world and time as he found appealing in the books he loved.

The things to which he was attracted—from goldmaking to Couperin—were remarkable in their disparity, and he brought to all of them an almost mystical devotion. But they reveal so little of his origin I have come to think of them as a screen before his birthplace; not for others, for himself.

The first time I saw Henry Wing, he was in the company of what I took to be women. I've mentioned that they may have been men, and, if we were speaking of someone other than Henry, a fondness for transvestites might be thought a quirk. Yet he himself saw nothing unusual in the company of men dressed as women.

It's not that he was naive, nor that he imagined transvestism widespread or widely accepted. (He lived in Ottawa, after all, a city whose surface disapproves of its own depths.) If anyone had bothered to ask why he chose such extraordinary company, as I later did, he would have answered, as he did, that it was good to be reminded of women in the company of men.[9]

Henry was not a restless or secretive man. He was at ease in his own eccentric world and, though both he and my mother had mellifluous voices, his was the texture of his being.

And so Henry and so Katarina . . .

During our first months with Henry Wing, Katarina sometimes said she found the man exhausting. She led me to believe we would be staying with Mr. Wing only until she could find work or until we could afford a place of our own. But, as always with my mother, words were an unfaithful guide to her feelings.

For one thing, she did not immediately set out to find work. She made a show of looking, certainly, getting up early to buy

---

[9] You know, it was Henry himself who told me that a number of the women who'd visited were men. I'd casually mentioned their extravagant perfumes when he told me. I wonder if he wasn't being facetious. I couldn't always understand his sense of humor.

the *Citizen* and settling down with it after breakfast. In those first months, it was as if her profession were Newspaper Reading. She wasn't ready to make coffee for men in suits, or to spend her days answering the telephone.

Given the times, and her lack of formal education, I'm amazed by her conviction that she could find anything better. What employment was there for women, save waiting on tables or answering telephones? Moreover, she was, at twenty-nine, a little old to enter the fray, and disinclined to sit by the door and greet the clients of Mr. Such and Such or the patients of Dr. So and So.

(Of course, my mother being the woman she was, I was not surprised when, in the end, she found work that was not exactly secretarial, and a workplace that, despite her lack of formal training, methodically rewarded her talent and enthusiasm: Revenue Canada.)

In the early days, before she found work, Henry would stay with her in the sitting room while she read the *Citizen*. He brought with him a silver tray with white handles; on the tray, a squat Florida-blue teapot and two white cups. Though she rarely drank it, he would pour for her while the tea was weak (burnt orange) and then wait until it was black before serving himself.

My mother usually sat, legs tucked under her, on the sofa. Henry stood by the fireplace, thinking, no doubt, about the place of this or that idea in the scheme of his cyclopedia. He could stand for hours, unmoving, contemplating, or, if there was reading to do, with an open book whose pages he leisurely turned.

The two of them together like that, in silence . . . it was both comforting and disturbing.

That winter, I'd pass the sitting room on my way out the door.

— Good-bye, I'd say. I'm going to school.

And they would both look my way, smiling.

The small mysteries of the scene affected me, long before I knew them for mysterious. How blue the teapot looked on its table beside the sofa, and how still my parents kept. Yes, and

1. How in the world did Henry make his living?
   (He had so much time for Katarina.)
2. What exactly did their silence mean?
   (Not silence in general, not wordlessness, but this particular silence, the quiet of these people in this room, morning after morning?)

The sensual details, the teapot, the white cups with steam rising from them, persist in my imagination. I don't know why the young Thomas was so affected by them. I remember the teapot, but it brings me none of the comfort it brought my younger self. It's a memory of comfort, now.

As for Henry's livelihood, it was, to an extent, mysterious, but it was even more banal. He bought and sold stocks, speculating on the market. He was a wondrously talented speculator, making a tidy fortune from relatively few hours' work, but "mysterious" isn't really the word for it.

And finally, as to silence, well . . . perhaps I made it more intricate than it was. I'm not as sensitive to it now, but for my younger self, peace of mind depended on the quality of silence that pervaded the sitting room. In those days, I thought I could tell the difference between silence and quiet, quiet and wordlessness, wordlessness and hush.

It was a question of sensing what had gone on just prior to my entrance on the scene.

Wordlessness was speaking without finding the words, a

language in the sound of crumpling newsprint, or the click of cup on saucer. For the first few months, Henry and my mother were wordless, or, rather, because he preceded her in intimacy, Henry was silent and my mother was wordless.

Silence was other than the absence of words, and other than the absence of sound; a state in which the rattling of a newspaper was insignificant. It was also something other than stillness. Movement was unimportant. The lifting of a teapot, the turning of a page, a suppressed yawn . . . all of these had no meaning in silence, though they had meaning in wordlessness, and meaning again in quiet.

After a time, Henry was quiet and my mother was silent.

Quiet took place in the possibility of words, of words just before silence or words just after. It was a wanting to speak or a wanting to have spoken, fraught with the expectation that comes when movement, or the disposition of a body, *might* have meaning. I mean, quiet was expecting or waiting, without words, for words (in one direction), and listening or attending, without words, after words (in the other).

Now, quiet I could live with. It was squarely in the realm of intimacy, a good sign. And, six or seven months after our arrival in Ottawa, when Henry was quiet and my mother was quiet, I could feel something like hush, the state for which I felt both hope and fear.

I'm embarrassed, now that it means so little to me, but in my imagination hush was something like being together, without need for words or silence, movement or stillness. It was the silence toward which all their silences tended.

You would think I'd be thrilled to catch them in such intimacy, and part of me *was* thrilled. The few occasions on which I discovered them like this, hushed, as I went out the front door, were almost enough to make me feel at home and reconcile me to being there.

Yet, it was this very reconciliation that made me anxious.

If you add the pressure of my anxieties to her already troubled circumstances, it seems miraculous that my mother ever managed to feel anything at all for Henry.

Still, in the summer of 1968, some twelve months after our abandonment in Manotick, I believe they were in love, in love despite me, despite their differences, despite Mrs. Williams.

I had kept close watch on them, furiously trying to interpret their words and actions, but, as it turns out, I had looked for all the wrong things. The moment I realized their feelings for each other had intensified, I was as surprised as if the two of them had only recently been strangers.

It was a Sunday morning, and we were in the dining room.

The morning itself was unusual. Mrs. Williams and I had gone for kaiser rolls from the bakery on Bank. As with every Sunday during Mrs. Williams's tenure, we ate buljol, but on this day I'd helped her prepare it.

The kitchen stank of salted cod. We'd thrown the leathery squares of codfish into a pot of boiling water, and when they'd boiled for some time we scooped them out, washed the scum from the pot, and then boiled the fish again.

While we waited for the fish, it was my task to cut the onions, tomatoes, and green peppers into small pieces. Mrs. Williams hard-boiled two eggs, and then, when everything was cooked, she drained the cod, pulled the flesh from the spines, and let it fall into a deep yellow bowl.

While the fish was still warm, she poured olive oil over it, and

I mixed everything (onions, tomatoes, peppers) together in the bowl so that my hands were slick and smelled edible.

It was a pleasure, this helping out. I felt close to Mrs. Williams. We juggled the kaiser rolls from the oven to a shallow wicker basket, one by one. And, when everything was ready, she sliced the eggs and arranged them carefully on the buljol.

I was proud of myself.

— That smells wonderful, my mother said as we brought the fish and rolls into the dining room.

— We have a talented young man with us, said Henry.

My mother smiled.

We?

That was the moment. Henry said "we" where previously there'd been only *I*, *You*, *Me*, *Tom*, *Thomas*, *Kata*, *Katarina*.

There was nothing intimate in their table manners. Henry ate as slowly as he always did. It took good timing to see him lift anything to his mouth. My mother ate as she always did, precisely; fork ready, one hand in her lap, fork charged, food taken, fork down, repeat.

But something had changed.

— Thank you, Mrs. Williams, my mother said at the end of the meal.

— You are mos' welcome, Miss MacMillan.

What exactly did Henry's "we" signify? Were the three of us to go on as family? And how did I feel about family, now that it was possible? It was one thing to imagine a warm life on Cooper, but what did I really think of Henry Wing? What, for that matter, did I really think of my mother?

What did I feel, beyond what I was duty-bound to feel?

At that moment, dawdling at the table, breaking my kaiser roll into the cod, I felt something like humiliation. I had yearned for . . . what, exactly?

But perhaps Henry had meant nothing by "we"... a slip of the tongue ... wishful thinking ... whistling in the dark ... As long as my mother and Henry's relations were ambiguous, I could live in hope of family, without family, a thing I knew little about.

Their relations weren't ambiguous for long.

In the days that followed, my mother and Henry were not quiet, not silent, not hushed; none of that. They spoke in a new register. Their pretexts for conversation—weather, dust, sun, etc.—were pretexts for saying "our weather," "our dust," "our sun," "our etc."

Yes, of course. There isn't a particle of earth insignificant to Love. I can say that with respect these days, but at the time it was disturbing to hear them speak intimately of things that didn't matter. I don't know which upset me most, their deeper feelings for each other, their new way of speaking, or the fact I'd missed the moment when they'd begun to love.

(I'm relating the thoughts of my younger self. For all I know, my mother never loved anyone but Henry Wing or loved Henry from the instant she met him, so that our stepping into 77 Cooper was already a crossing into Love.)

The two of them even looked different. Henry, whom I'd always thought handsome, was more so now; stiller, not at all ridiculous. My mother, her face beautiful, her brown eyes wider, her eyebrows darker ... everything about her gentler and good-humored, when she wasn't around Mrs. Williams. She even wore dresses. In particular, there was a simple knee-length paisley shift that made her look, well, female.

And yes, of course I have felt something like the oedipal thing for my mother, but I've never desired her in the way that, say, I desire you. It was into a world of fear, not desire, that her shift dress threw me, an abyss more religious than sexual, God help me. I mean, it was more upsetting that my mother might become sexual than that she was so. *Nuance.*

Actually, I wonder if their appearances changed in fact, or for me alone. At this point, the question is unanswerable, but the other witness to their love, Mrs. Williams, expressed an anxiety similar to mine.

— Is like Miss MacMillan goin' an' marry Mr. Wing? she said one day.

We were both in the kitchen, she making bread and I looking through a book called *Della Francesca ou les ébats de l'amour.* The title is what attracted me; though, in all the years I've known the book, I've only managed to admire the illustrations, the text being too difficult for anyone but Henry.

(Not that all of Henry's books were so obscure about the nature of love. After his death, I found a number of exotic volumes, from *Les Délices des coeurs*, by Ahmad al-Tifachi, to *Thérèse Philosophe*, by Anonymous, in a dusty white bookcase beneath his bedroom window.)

— Ent? Mrs. Williams asked.

— I guess so, I answered.

I pushed *Les ébats* toward Mrs. Williams and pointed to one of its illustrations.

— Look at this, I said.

Perhaps she felt she'd gone too far in asking me about my mother. She took the book from me. Her fingers stuck to the pages. She brought it closer with her wrists. She leaned over the page, then pushed the book away.

— Very pretty, she said.

Some four or five months later, when I accused her of taking my mother's shoes, Mrs. Williams said

— It ain' true.

And Henry answered

— I'm very sorry, Hilda . . . I'm afraid you'll have to leave us.

What else could he have said?

In the world of Romantic Love, it didn't matter if my mother was lying. It mattered only that she was Henry's beloved, and that her very presence, being Love, was also Truth.

In that world, it really didn't matter that I had not seen Mrs. Williams steal. I could have accused Mrs. Williams of anything at all, of witchcraft, say, or of setting fire to the Parliament buildings. So long as my mother gave thumbs-down, it was all over for Mrs. Williams.

Nor was there any room for Mrs. Williams to maneuver. If she had said

— Is all true. Is I self take Miss MacMillan shoes

there would have been even less to talk about. There was no court on whose mercy she could depend. There was only my mother, and my mother wanted her gone.

— Thank you, Henry, my mother said when Mrs. Williams was banished.

And Henry answered

— You're welcome, Kata

as if it had been possible for him to transgress the laws of their intimate world.

And where exactly did this "intimate world" leave me?

It left me nowhere.

Not right away, but soon after Mrs. Williams's departure, I began to see that the thing I'd wished for, this intimacy between Henry and Katarina, had nothing to do with me. I felt insignificant in their little universe of Sun and Satellite. The two of them didn't need me. Their happiness didn't depend on me the way mine depended on them.

I was wrong to think this way, of course. The proof of their love for me was everywhere. It was in the way they spoke to me, the way Henry put his arm around my shoulders, the way my mother touched my hair, patting it down before I left for school. How could they have loved all the particles of earth without loving me? Still, I took all their fuss for condescension.

And so, perhaps in revenge or self-defense or frustration, I began to steal.

It was thrilling.

I had no intentions as such, no conscious motives. There was something pure in my thieving, something so far beyond my ability to understand, it was as if I weren't stealing at all.

It wasn't like collecting beetles, which I'd begun to do seriously. Every beetle I caught was carefully set in the display case Henry had made for me; every one was there for a reason, from ladybug to firefly.

There was no rationale for the things I stole. They brought me no satisfaction. I stole mainly from my mother, though I wasn't conscious of trying to hurt her in particular. I neither sold nor used most of the things I took. I hid everything, save for the money I stole from Henry. I used that to buy comics.

It might seem to you that theft was an obvious choice for my "revenge." And so it was, though my eleven-year-old self wasn't entirely conscious of what he was doing. When the time came, when Henry and my mother could no longer hide their feelings, when Mrs. Williams was banished, it simply felt appropriate to steal.

The first thing I took was a change purse.

I took it while Henry and my mother were in the sitting

room. They were both on the sofa, drinking tea, listening to Couperin, no doubt, quietly talking about something or other.

(In those days they talked about Elgin Public, Revenue Canada, Henry's books and his great project, the state of the house, paint needed here or perhaps wallpaper there, the furniture, which my mother thought too old-fashioned, a car, though Henry had never learned to drive, my mother's clothes, which Henry thought not altogether worthy of her beauty, my clothes, which I outgrew so quickly they despaired of keeping me covered . . . meaningless prattle, as far as I could tell.)

I was sitting with them, idly listening, when I decided to go upstairs for a book.

— You're off, Tom? Henry asked.

— I'm going to get a book.

— What are you reading, Tom?

— I don't know, I answered.

— You don't know what you're reading, sweetheart?

(As if I were her sweetheart.)

— I'm sorry, Tom. I didn't mean to be inquisitive.

— Bring your book down, Thomas. You can read it with us.

— Okay . . . fine.

I went up the stairs as slowly as I could, not at all eager to return to their company. I may even have counted all of the banister's uprights, something I liked to do anyway. (There are 33, 34, or 35 of them in all, 22 to the second floor, unless you count the first bole, which I rarely did, and 11 to the third, unless ditto, which ditto, except for variety.)

For some reason, the door to my mother's bedroom was ajar. That was unusual. She usually kept her door locked. I listened for footsteps and then, more by curiosity than design, I went into her room.

This wasn't the first time I'd been in the room, but it was evening and dark, and I had to turn on the lights to make my way around. The room was neat and spare. My mother's bed, as wide and long as my own, was against the wall, with its smooth white coverlet, the brass headboard smelling of the polish she used to keep it clean. The room itself smelled of her perfume and of the perfumed powder she kept on the chest of drawers beside the bed.

Her handbag was beside the powder box and, again curious, I looked into it: lipstick, a nail file, Kleenex, hairpins, eyeliner . . . the usual things, I imagine, but so many of them that the inside of the purse was a small chaos.

At the bottom of the handbag, there was a wallet and a change purse. There were dollar bills in the wallet. I instinctively thought to take the money, but I had the change purse in hand when I heard a silence.

The music had stopped. I panicked. I snapped the handbag shut, put the change purse in my pants pocket, turned the lights in the room off, closed the door, opened it again, leaving it ajar, as I'd found it.

My retreat must have taken less than thirty seconds. I was terrified I'd left some clue to my presence. Going quickly back to my room, I chose a worthy book, something to impress, if either of them still wanted me to read: once again, *Les ébats de l'amour*, by Henri Serres, a book that has had a singular influence on my life, though I've never read it through.

I walked down the stairs, oversize book in my arms and, unwittingly, my mother's change purse in my pocket.

As I entered the sitting room, my mother said

— That was quick.

— I was reading, I answered.

— What's the book?

— *Della Francesca ou les ébats de l'amour.*

— *Les ébats de l'amour?* That's . . . nice. Why don't you read to us?

— Do I have to?

— Please?

I made a show of annoyance, then sat on the floor, cross-legged, the book open in my lap. The change purse slipped a little, so I kept one hand on the book and the other on my pocket, to keep the purse from falling out entirely.

> "*Le visage de sa mère était d'une pâleur effrayante.*
>
> — *O mon pauvre Pierre! Pourquoi ne fusses-tu né ailleurs, ou dans un temps moins amer?*
>
> *Le nouveau né, comme s'il avait compris son erreur, hurlait avec toute la force de ses poumons . . .*"
>
> *Façon assez particulière de décrire la naissance du mathématicien-peintre, n'est-ce pas? Mais c'est avec ce cri du peintre que commence le roman de Giocomo San Benedetto . . .*

I read on to the end of the chapter, scarcely understanding a word.

— That was very good, Henry said.

— Can I go to bed now?

— It's still early. Aren't you feeling well?

— I'm tired.

— Go ahead, Thomas. I'll be up in a minute.

No sooner had I left the room than I regretted leaving. I couldn't hear what they were saying, but I wanted to. I imagined they were talking about me. Could they tell I'd taken my mother's purse? Was there still time to put it back?

Once upstairs I was too distraught to wipe my face or brush my teeth. I hid the change purse under my mattress, pushing it as far to the center as I could.

— I'll be up in a minute, my mother had said.

But I waited an eternity, convinced they knew everything, desperately trying to decide if I had time to put the change purse back. When I heard my mother coming up the stairs, I was ready to confess all or, as seemed wiser, to say: Mother, I think this fell out of your handbag. I kept it safe for you.

As it happened, she spoke first.

— Sorry I took so long.

She sat beside me on the bed.

— Thomas, she began, Henry and I have been talking.

I was convinced she knew about the purse.

— We've been thinking . . . maybe you haven't been reading the right things.

— Reading? I asked.

— If it were up to Henry, you could read anything at all.

Now this was entirely unexpected. I felt relieved, confused, exhilarated, and, once I realized what she was talking about, slightly indignant. What about my reading? Had Henry told her about *Les Bijoux indiscrets*? The book *was* unusual, but, after all, it was the first book to spark my interest in Latin and . . . I had learned something . . . and . . .

No, it wasn't Diderot who upset her. It was Henri Serres.

— You're too young to understand what you're reading.

— But . . .

— Just listen to me, please.

We had never spoken of sex. She was uncomfortable. Not that sex was a bad thing, no, no, but it was not straightforward. I would soon encounter sensations that were perfectly normal, but they both felt it would be better if I had a guide to them, and it would be best if the guide shared my plumbing.

— My plumbing?

— Yes, dear.

Which is why Henry was going to help me with the facts of life. He'd persuaded her it would be wrong to curb my curiosity, but, at least until Henry and I had spoken, she thought I should read something other than books for adults.

Despite the relief I felt at having my theft undiscovered, I was irritated by their injustice. I mean, as far as I could tell, *Les ébats* was not at all risqué. Hadn't she listened to my reading? Or was the title alone enough to set off parental alarms?

— But . . .

— Never mind, Thomas. We'll talk about this later.

And that was the end of it. Seeing *Les ébats* on the night table beside me, she took it away, until such time as . . .

Henry's task was far from easy.

How *does* one explain the mysteries of human sexuality to an eleven-year-old? I had learned the theory behind intercourse and conception and, thanks to the magazines I'd read in Petrolia, I had a pretty good idea how the first part of the process would look.

This wasn't supposed to be a lecture on mechanics, though. Once one has said "penis" and "vagina" and remarked on their suiteness, one for the other, the physical mysteries are more or less resolved.

No, Henry's talk was to be about the complications that arise from conjunction.

It might have been easier for him, and better for me, if my

mother had allowed the two of us to deal with this alone. Instead, she insisted on participating as an "interested observer."

A week or so after I'd stolen her change purse, my mother put some cookies on a saucer, filled a glass with milk, and shepherded me to the library, where Henry waited.

— Why don't you sit here? he said, his hand on the back of an armchair.

My mother sat on a chair he'd brought for her, and when she had settled on the edge of it, Henry began.

— The world is a biological entity, Tom, as you know . . . or do you?

— Yes, I know.

— Wonderful. So you know we're not so different from beetles and toads?

— I guess so.

— Good. There's not much else to say, really.

— What do you mean there's nothing else? my mother asked.

— I mean, regeneration is the key, in a manner of speaking.

— Don't use vague words.

— I apologize, my love. Do you understand regeneration, Tom?

— I guess so.

— Don't guess, Thomas. What Henry means is that all creatures reproduce and so do we.

— I know that, I answered.

— Good. Go on, Henry.

— Well, Tom, the chief difference between animals and ourselves is that although the reproductive act is physically uncomplicated for both, it is psychologically complex for human beings . . .

— And emotionally complex, my mother added.

— Yes, emotionally as well . . .

— And why is it emotionally complex? my mother prompted.

— Because it is a matter of custom, ritual, and group conduct . . .

— No, my mother said.

Henry paused to consider where he might have gone off course.

— It generally requires more than a single participant, he said.

— No, my mother repeated. It's complex because it's a matter of trust.

— Yes, I see, said Henry, waiting for her to go on.

And when she didn't

— It's a matter of trust, Tom, and trust is complex. Let's say you were a farmer in Hornpayne, where the ground is generally stony and it's difficult to make things grow. But *your* fields are rich and you could grow whatever you wanted: cherries, wheat, lemons . . .

To this day I sometimes remember Henry like this: looking down at me, unruffled by the situation, convinced that such mysteries as could be resolved were trivial; those that could not, essential. It wasn't in his nature to dispel mystery, but he could lead me to it.

— . . . wheat, lemons, grapefruit . . . anything you wanted, but you need the help of another person. You understand?

— Yes, I answered.

— Wouldn't you want someone with whom you could work?

— I guess so.

— What does this have to do with passion, Henry?

— Well, Kata, I was about to suggest that, in Hornpayne, the only way to find someone who will help with the land is to offer her half the property.

— Why? my mother asked.

(I couldn't have answered that question if my life depended on it.)

— Let us say that *that* is the way people are in Hornpayne . . .

— But you could hire someone, my mother suggested.

— Not in *this* Hornpayne, Kata. In this Hornpayne, you have to choose your partner wisely. It wouldn't do to give half one's land to just anyone. And remember, it's a condition of life in Hornpayne that one must surrender half one's property to attract a partner and to have one's fields flourish . . .

They bickered, gently, on the course Henry had chosen. Though my mother appreciated the subtlety of his model, she was convinced it was lost on me. Besides, she thought Henry's approach overly mercantile, a cavil he answered by reminding her that the messenger of the gods (Hermes) was also the god of merchants, a bit of information that reassured her, though it plunged me even further into confusion.

By the time Henry returned to his parable and elaborated on fertility and responsibility, I was more interested in incidentals than message: my mother's attitude, Henry's voice, her face, his hands, the waning light, the taste of oatmeal cookies, my fingers wet from the glass of milk I held.

After a long while, Henry asked

— Do you see?

— Oh, yes, I answered.

And, rising from her chair, my mother said

— Thank you, Henry.

She put out her hand, palm up. From the shelf behind him Henry took down *Les ébats*. He gave her the book.

— Here you are, Thomas, she said.

If they had asked me to prove I understood Henry's lecture, I'd have failed miserably. I was even more confused about the mysteries of sexuality, though now I understood there was something to understand. Perhaps that was the point.

Or, it may be that Henry's words were meant for my mother as much as they were for me. My mother understood and appreciated them better than I did, or seemed to, and she was satisfied. Little enough reason to allow an eleven-year-old the run of Henry's library, but the effect wasn't all bad. The further association of sex and books made an even more avid reader of me.

— Thank you, Mother, I said.

Despite Hornpayne, or despite the trust they showed me, I went on stealing. What's worse, I felt a growing addiction to the activity itself.

Sometime after taking my mother's angora sweater, I even stopped worrying about excuses. I had successfully taken so many things by then, it seemed useless to think up lies I wouldn't use. Not once did either of them show any sign they suspected me of theft.

It was wonderful to sneak about, listening for their voices, for the sound of footsteps, for the creak of the staircase, and wonderful to answer

— No, I haven't seen your dress

or

— No, I haven't seen your stickpin

when they asked me about their missing things.

Very few acts have given me as much pleasure. It was exciting to discover how easily Henry and my mother were deceived. Their vulnerability was exciting, and perhaps, in the end, I continued to steal for the sake of those brief but fantastic moments when I watched one or the other looking helplessly for some lost object.

And yet, I was not a good thief.

If it took them months to discover the connection between me and their vanishing things, it was, to begin with, because I took things it made no sense for me to take. Over the space of some five months, I took

> change purse, shoe, necklace, ring, magazine, socks, money, blanket, shirt, handbag, rose water, dress, orchid, cuff links, orrery, monocle, earrings, abacus, gloves, angora sweater, identity card, nail polish, gold chain, bookmark, ink, stickpin, pants, undershirt, tambourine, talcum, nail file, handkerchief, hat.

In my neatest hand, I wrote each item on the back pages of *Treasure Island*. Beside each I noted the day and the date it was taken. (I still have the book. It is open before me now. I had a tendency to take things on Tuesdays and Thursdays.)

I allowed just enough time to pass between excursions, enough time for my mother or Henry to forget previous losses. My mother asked after her ring, her sweater, her dress, and her identity card, but nothing else. Henry seemed unaware that his abacus, his monocle, or his cuff links were missing.

This timing was a matter of timidity rather than design. I didn't choose my moments as a real thief would.

And, finally, my choice of hiding places was inept. On several occasions, when I returned to see if a thing were safe, I couldn't find it. Henry's miniature orrery, for instance, I'd hidden behind a box in the attic. Some time after hiding it, I went up to admire the planets, but I couldn't find the orrery at all. I pushed the boxes about, feeling around in them—crammed with books, all of them, barely space enough for my small hands.

Thinking Henry had found me out, I panicked.

And yet, the next time I saw him, perhaps moments after sneaking down from the attic, Henry gave no sign that he knew anything. Had my mother discovered it, then? Perhaps she'd seen me squirreling the planets up to the attic? Not a sign from her, either.

I was rattled enough to stop taking things for a while, but then I stole Henry's monocle (and broke it), my mother's faux ruby earrings, Henry's abacus, my mother's leather gloves, her angora sweater . . . all as if the orrery's disappearance were a fluke.

The orrery was, of all the things I stole, the only one I actually coveted. In my memory, it is exquisite: a glass square in which there was a model of the solar system (minus Pluto). Eight concentric wire ellipses moved out like ripples from the sun, a glass bead on each. The planets were colored marbles; the sun canary yellow and translucent.

The mechanism that drove the planets in their course was wound by a brass mouse-ear key that is the only part of the orrery I still have.

I'm almost certain Henry recovered the orrery from the attic. There was no one else to miss it. Still, as I haven't seen it since 1969, I suspect it was well and truly stolen by one of the men he later hired to keep house. In which case, I'm glad I kept the key. It would be difficult to replace, with its heptagonal eye, and one of the chief pleasures of this orrery was the music it made as the marbles moved in their orbits.

It was carelessness that put an end to this episode of my childhood.

I'd have been found out eventually, of course, but my sneaking around, the book in which I noted what I'd stolen, even the sheer number of things I stole . . . none of these were responsible for my downfall.

I'd begun to treat the whole thing casually. I walked into any room I found open, taking whatever caught my eye, no longer listening for footsteps, for creaking staircases, for soft voices.

By the time I stole my mother's hat, I'd begun to find my own behavior tiresome, without, for all that, being able to stop myself. After taking some thirty-odd things, it was as if I could go on stealing indefinitely, with ever diminishing returns.

But . . .

One night, I took to arranging my mother's clothes under the mattress of my bed. It had occurred to me that I'd taken enough of her things to make a version of her, dress first, sweater over dress, gloves where hands should be, handbag on one of the gloves, necklace on sweater, hat (beret) above the necklace, and earrings where her ears should be.

Though the mattress was heavy, I let it rest on my shoulder and did my best to smooth everything out on the box spring: dress, sweater, gloves, hat. The game was so amusing, I lost track of time. It was especially difficult to keep the sweater unrumpled, to smooth its arms out to their full length.

I was standing there with the mattress on my shoulder when I heard someone coming up the stairs. I let the mattress fall, pushed it into place with my hip, and dove under the covers.

— Time for bed, Thomas.

It was my mother.

— All right, I said.

Smiling, she sat down beside me.

— And how was your day?

— It was okay.

— Tell me, she said.

I couldn't think of anything to say. My heart was racing; my mind was on alert, fabricating reasons for the clothes under my mattress.

— Are we going to stay with Henry, now?

The same question I'd been asking for months.

— For a while, she answered.

— What did you do today? I asked.

She was looking down at the floor. I shook her arm.

— What did you do?

— What's this?

She bent down to pull at the sleeve of her sweater.

— What's this doing here?

She sounded pleased to find it.

— Oh, I said. I was cold.

She stood up.

— I only borrowed it.

As she pulled the sweater free, the sleeve of her dress and the handle of her purse came with it.

— Get up, Thomas.

— Why?

— Get out of the bed, please. What's all this?

Now she wasn't pleased. She was perplexed as she pulled everything out from under my mattress. Her son had hidden various pieces from her wardrobe in his room. What must she have thought?

The strangeness of my own behavior suddenly struck me. I'd had no particular motive for taking things. As far as I could tell, I'd stolen without plan, without intention. Yet I felt humiliated, aware of something unnameable but not quite unfamiliar.

I'm not sure it occurred to her that my sin was only theft.

— Did you take all this?

— Yes, I answered.

— Why?

I would normally have been too embarrassed to face her, but, in a moment of inspiration, or damnation, I looked up and, with a sincerity I've rarely summoned, even when telling the truth, I said

— Henry told me to.

— Henry? Why would Henry tell you to take my clothes?

And again, with sincerity

— He wanted to buy you others ... he never liked your clothes.

— That's ridiculous.

And now, on the verge of tears

— I'm sorry, Mother ... I know I shouldn't have ...

I don't think she believed me, but the idea that Henry was trying to manipulate her must have struck a chord. Besides, given the things she'd discovered (shoes, necklace, dress, etc.), my lie would have been a relief. I mean, if you rule out motiveless theft and sexual deviance, very few explanations could reasonably encompass my behavior.

— Why wouldn't he ask me himself?

— I know I shouldn't have, I repeated.

I lowered my head, repentant.

— We'll talk about this tomorrow, she said.

She didn't hurry out, but she left the room, distracted: door open, lights on. I stood for a long time waiting for her return, trying to decide if I should close the door myself.

Now, what were the chances of a story like that holding up?

I don't mean to diminish my guilt, but, to my knowledge, there is no world in which Henry could have behaved as I said he had. He had only to say, "I think cloth in general unworthy of you, Kata, but I'd have taken your clothes myself if I were going to take them," and there was an end to my lie.

So, when my mother called me into the sitting room the next evening, I expected the worst.

On, or draped about, the sofa were the things she'd found under my mattress. My mother stood by the fireplace, and I stood near the sofa, until, after a while, Henry entered, bringing with him a tray laden with cups, milk, cookies, and a teapot. He smiled as he offered them to me, but it was painful to look him in the face.

— Would you like anything, Kata?

— No, thank you, she answered.

— So, Henry asked, what's the occasion?

(She hadn't told him?)

— I found these things hidden in Thomas's room, my mother said.

— Did you?

— Thomas says you asked him to take them.

Pause, and then

— I asked him to take them?

— Yes. Did you?

Standing beside the sofa, still as a mouse, I passed the most excruciating moments of my childhood; the final moments, actually. Henry said

— Tom told you?

— Yes.

— Then I admit it, he said softly. Yes.

I looked up in disbelief. He was looking down at me, not smiling, but not unkindly either. I thought he must have misunderstood the question.

— You asked my son to sneak around my room and take my clothes? How could you?

— I'm sorry, he answered.

— Why didn't you tell me you hated my clothes?

Pause, and then

— Tom told you I hated your clothes?

— Of course.

— I'm sorry, Kata.

My mother stood unmoving and silent for some time before she said

— Thomas, what you did was wrong. Leave us, please.

That was the last moment when I might have admitted to lying. Henry stood at the other side of the fireplace, hands behind his back, graceful, placid.

It hurt me to keep quiet, but I wanted them to suffer now that it had come to suffering. I walked slowly from the sitting room and slowly up the stairs, trying to catch the particulars of their contretemps, but there was only silence.

Looking back on it now, I can't imagine a more unhappy confluence of elements.

My mother, though she clearly loved Henry, could not stand the idea of being manipulated. She may not have believed me when I said Henry was trying to play her, but his confession would have been enough to instill doubt where none could be tolerated.

And then: myself at twelve.

And finally: Henry.

I still don't know what to make of Henry. He was either ridiculous or admirable, depending. I sometimes think he acted out of consideration for me, that he wished to spare me the humiliation. That's quite Henry.

It may also be that he thought he couldn't expose me without hurting my mother. It would have been painful for Kata to know her son for the thief and liar I was at twelve. He would have wanted to spare her that, and so he fell on the sword. And that too is Henry.

Whichever it is, Henry ridiculous or Henry admirable, he never held this moment against me, never wavered in his kindness. In that, he was perhaps unintentionally cruel, because it has taken me years to forgive myself.

I mean, I only now see my behavior for what it was, and I am sorry that, although this wasn't the end of Henry and Katarina's living together, it was the end's beginning.

XII

——

Over the past few months, my life seems to have become both simple and complex. It is outwardly simple.

7 o'clock:	Wake, wash, eat.
9 o'clock:	Write, with a break for Alexander.
11 o'clock:	More of the same (write, write).
1 o'clock (P.M.):	Write my letters to the *Citizen*.
3 o'clock (P.M.):	Promenade, walk, think of you.
5 o'clock (P.M.):	If I have gone to the library, I return, my head filled with words.
7 o'clock (P.M.):	The usual (read, wash), and I wonder should I call your number again.
9 o'clock (P.M.):	Feed Alexander. Food, for me, if possible.
11 (P.M.) to 7 (A.M.):	Sleep.

It is complex in that the writing I do brings me a little closer to the dead but no closer to the living. It brings me closer to myself at times, but I have not always been my favorite place . . .

It's been a year since my mother died, a shade less since Henry passed. This spasm of memory has just about run its course, I think.

I had broken the back of my own childhood.

I was twelve when I turned away from the cloistered world of Henry and Katarina.

Their relationship survived my thieving and my lies. It went on for months, but my feelings for the two of them died. I thought I knew their frailties and, unforgiving as one can only be at twelve, I began to think them unworthy of respect.

It may have been self-defense that turned me away from them, away from any family that might spring up around them. It may also have been self-punishment or impenitence or a hardening of the heart, but, whatever it was, I was no longer interested.

It wasn't as if I suddenly found myself free, you understand, or even that, at twelve, I knew what freedom might be. Not at all. I was still unable to do without "belonging," but I had discovered a "somewhere else" more hospitable than their "there."

Ottawa, the City Itself

My mother and Henry were both out of place in Ottawa.

My mother lasted some twenty years in the city, without ever feeling at home. She moved around, living here and there, looking for a place that felt other than temporary. But, though she bought a house at Osgood and Henderson, she moved back to Petrolia, of all places, in 1990.

Henry's life and circumstances I've already described. Though he was at home, you could not have said he was at home in Ottawa, or not exactly. His home was elsewhere in time, one in which Lampman and Scott might have taken tea. But they were only ghosts in the city I discovered.

For me, Ottawa was tall and busy, various shades of ash, green, blue, and brown. It was, once I'd adjusted to its scale, so vivid that I'm astounded there was ever a time it meant nothing to me. It has been everything to me since: my ocean, my desert, my plain.

I threw myself into the arms of the city, and though cities aren't made to keep you company, Ottawa was what I needed for respite. Besides, I rarely went out on my own. My companions, or those I remember, were François Gagné and Lucie Lefebvre, who went to Garneau though they lived close by, and Andrew Haller, who lived at Cooper and Metcalfe and went to Elgin Public.

As you can imagine, I had no talent for happiness, and not much for friendship, but Lucie and François were unusual in ways I found disarming, and Andrew actually shared my interest in beetles. I remember our time together as agreeable; though, for the most part, I couldn't tell you what we did.

I was with Lucie and François when I first encountered Ottawa-as-Ottawa, before it was Ottawa-as-Thomas.

Months after Henry had fallen on the sword, Lucie and I followed the Canal to Rideau.

The day was warm. The water in the canal was sky blue. We walked together, talking about something or other, when I suddenly noticed we were surrounded by people, all of them strolling along the promenade. And I was happy to be with so many. We went to the river and then up the steps, on along Rideau Street to the Market.

At the Market, there were so many people, it was like drifting on a tide. The place smelled of fish, of cheese, of apples and cucumbers, tomatoes and green peppers, and, by the cages, of chicken shit.

It was on this day that I saw a man take a chicken from its cage of wooden slats and wring its neck in one graceful motion, bird by the neck, a flick of the wrist. I was sorry for the chicken, but it was so artfully killed there was necessity in its sacrifice.

It was also on this day that I saw a German shepherd pounce on a rat that had run out from the back of a shop. The dog shook its head violently from side to side with the rat in its mouth. I took a stick and chased the dog away, but when I went back to see if the rat were alive, the poor thing bit me and scuttled away, finding protection under a wooden pallet.

I felt such concern for the rat, I didn't notice my hand was bleeding until Lucie started to cry. And then, for weeks afterward, I worried obsessively about rabies. I didn't say a thing to either Henry or my mother. Instead, thinking the first sign of infection would be hydrophobia, I avoided water and drank milk and apple juice.

I know it's odd that moments like these should have drawn me to the city, but the day was an adventure, and the city is vivid in my memory: blue, green, and gray.

My second encounter with Ottawa was even more banal.

François and I walked far from home on a summer day. Far for us, anyway; along Elgin to Laurier, over the Laurier Bridge, past the university, which sprawled for blocks, its buildings mysterious and inviting, on all the way to Strathcona.

We were arguing about who was better, Concombre Masqué or Iznogoud, Tintin or Jonny Quest. I didn't care about any of them, really. I preferred *Spiderman*, which François had never read. In fact, I had brought along an issue of *Spiderman*, rolled tight, the sweat of my palm smudging the ink on its cover.

I knew that François's English wasn't good enough for him to read the comic on his own, so I was determined to read it for him. It somehow offended me that he should not know J. Jonah

Jameson or Peter Parker. It bothered me that he didn't know Tony Stark or Reed Richards, either, but I couldn't show him everything at once.

François and I wandered around the park, from one end to the other, attracted by the noise of a ball game, discreetly following two teenagers, a boy and a girl walking hand in hand, who stopped every hundred yards or so to embrace.

We must have spent hours wasting time and watching the river, so that, when we finally sat down by the rapids, it was late afternoon.

I unfurled my *Spiderman* and smoothed it on my lap. Then, pausing only to admire the drawings, I translated each of the speech balloons.

François was enthralled.

— C'est qui Doctor Octopus?

— C'est un méchant . . .

— Oh! 'Garde-donc ses bras d' pieuvre!

I read it to him twice before the sun sank too low, the streetlamps came on, and it was time to go.

— J't'en supplie, Thomas, prête-le moi, he begged as we walked home.

— Mais tu ne lis pas l'anglais . . .

— J't'en supplie.

And I gave him the comic, knowing I wouldn't see it again, not this copy. The waning sunlight, and the way Parliament looked from the bridge, and the soft light of the streetlamps, it was these things that bred a kindness in me.

— Okay, I said, garde-le.

Both of those excursions, with Lucie in the Market and with François in Strathcona, were like moments in the world after a time in darkness. I mean, I was conscious of not being myself in a place that included me. I mean, I was briefly, blessedly, unselfconscious, and that was how I came to recognize home.

All of this, this turning toward Ottawa, is difficult to describe, because I wasn't turning toward or, at least, I wouldn't have said I was turning toward the city any more than I would have admitted to turning away from Henry's house. Yet, I turned.

How should I put this? You wouldn't say a heliotrope knows light, but it moves toward light, and it was the same for me.

Was Ottawa my light, then?

Yes and no.

At first it was a wilderness, and then it was my wilderness, and then it wasn't wilderness at all. I came to know it intimately, from Elgin and Cooper out, in waves.

The act of discovery was my light. Although Ottawa was the principal thing illuminated, it was through Ottawa, or with it, or in it, that I found my bearings away from my mother and Henry, and without them.

You see what I mean?

Ten years passed during which the outside world mattered more to me than mother, father, home and hearth. I made a concerted effort to put distance between myself and my childhood.

Not that I was successful.

The Years with Henry

I often wonder why Henry's feelings for my mother were not enough to keep them together.

It was reckless of him to admit having coerced me into theft, but it's unlikely a strong relationship would have foundered on such a small snag. Even if he had convinced me to steal her clothes, my mother should have forgiven him, if she really had been in love, and I have reason to believe she was in love with Henry.

(I'm assuming, as I always do, that cohabitation is a necessary complement to love, an expression of affection. Having had no real home of my own for most of my early years, I am sometimes despondent about the home I missed when Henry and my mother separated. I blame myself for a failure that may not have been a failure. It was only I who needed them to live together, after all. Their relationship continued, in its own way, until the end of their lives, and yet . . .)

Their separation, if that's what you call it, was not bitter.

One day, my mother and I went out to look at an apartment. We'd gone out to look for apartments often enough for me to think the occasion unremarkable. I was bored.

The apartment building, near Bank and Cooper, was not far from Henry's home. It was old and gray, exceptional only for its metal balconies, so rusty they looked as though they might clatter down at any time.

It was a little better inside, but not much: yellow walls, tall ceilings, two large bedrooms, big windows. It smelled sour, though, and the kitchen was small. We paced about the empty rooms for a while, but I assumed she'd say what she always said

— Thank you. I don't think so.

Instead, she turned to the landlord, a man about whom I remember only the Brylcreem.

— Two hundred is expensive, she said. I'll give you one-fifty. And that was it.

— What about Henry? I asked.

— He has his own home, she answered.

Nor was Henry surprised when she told him we were moving.

— Is there enough room for the two of you? he asked.

When the day came to move, he helped us. The three of us carried cardboard boxes along Cooper. We had little to take, my mother and I. In two years, I'd acquired a few more clothes and dozens of books. My mother may have had a few more things than I, but not many.

In fact, the only real inequity was in sleeping quarters. My mother had bought a bed for herself, but there was none for me.

Henry offered to buy one or to give us the bed I'd been sleeping in, but rather than take his money my mother suggested—*she* suggested—I stay with Henry until she could afford a bed for me. After all, our new home was so close to Henry's it would not be like living apart. And it was only temporary, you see.

— If that's what you want . . . , said Henry.

They looked to me, perhaps expecting some protest.

— I don't care, I said.

Not that I wouldn't have preferred to live with my mother. I had mixed feelings for Henry, guilt mostly, yet I wasn't about to show my feelings to either of them.

(I could never bring myself to return any of the things I'd stolen and, over time, lost most of them.)

— Then it's settled, said my mother.

The problem of my lodging was settled, yes, and, though I was not happy, this new arrangement turned out for the best.

To begin with, though it took only four months for her to buy me a bed, by the time she did, I was so comfortable with Henry I continued to sleep at his home almost as often as I did at hers. During those first months, I saw her almost every day. She spent most of her early evenings with us and, when she left for the night, Henry left me to my own devices. That freedom was more than compensation for the loss of my mother's company.

And it was in these months that my bond with Henry was mended.

These years with Henry, from 1969 to 1978, are even more sketchy than the first two. I find it difficult to recall specific moments, their sequence, or the emotions they provoked.

For the first few days, I lived in dread of confrontation, convinced that Henry would reprove me for the lies I'd told, but there was not a word, not a sign. It was as if the whole thing had happened to someone other than Henry, or had been perpetrated by someone other than me.

Instead, it was now that Henry told me about his own childhood: his parents' death, his lonely days, rain from a blue sky, the green skin of a coconut, and the ocean, the ocean, the ocean . . . He made himself less threatening, less adult.

We returned to the lab together, for the first time since the fiasco with gold. Here too he treated me as something of an equal, and though our work was less dramatic than goldmaking, it was more engaging in the long run.

I still had the periodic table memorized, and I was just as fascinated by the elements, so it was relatively easy for him to teach me simple equations, the first being

$$2H_2 + O_2 \rightarrow 2H_2O$$

(each side of the equation with its proper complement of atoms, nothing lost).

Over the years, when we weren't talking about his childhood, or playing at chemistry, we spoke about life, from birth to death, by way of books.

— You should read *Gravida*, he suggested one day when we were discussing dreams.

And off we went to find the Jensen.

The search for a book was inevitably as interesting as the book itself. We'd spend hours rummaging, pulling bright books from the shelves as we made our way through the library. For every *Gravida*, there was a Herodotus, a Marco Polo, a *Natural History of Selborne*.

Henry's art was in guiding me to things that might be of abiding interest. I was already in the habit of reading anything that looked as if it would give the slightest pleasure, but over the years I was tactfully directed to things I'd missed.

To this day there are books I can't pick up without thinking of Henry:

> *Flatland* (I was 12 when I read it)
> *Gravida* (14)
> *The Curves of Life* (16)
> *The Brothers Karamazov* (18)
> *Le parti pris des choses* (18)
> *The Figure in the Carpet* (20)

And once I'd finished a book, we would sit and talk about this character or that idea, about Fibonacci or a life in ten dimensions.

When we talked, I was usually the more tendentious, but Henry treated my opinions with respect, demurring only once when I called Smerdyakov good, but misguided.

— Don't you feel for the dogs? he asked gently.

The only real arguments we had came not over literature but science. I could not find it in myself to respect the errors of great men. Aristotle's version of biology struck me as ludicrous, and, yes, I could see the point of Lamarck's flower-collecting, but I felt, or had learned, disdain for *acquired characteristics*, and, as to Hegel, well . . . what wasn't impenetrable was rubbish and I, at twenty, wouldn't have fed his *Philosophy of Nature* to a pig.

I take that all back now, of course, though as to Hegel, well . . . I'm still inclined to spare the pigs.

I don't know that reading has helped me to live. I'm not certain it has prepared me for death, either, though Henry often mentioned that *that* was learning's only good. I do know that, at twenty, I began to tire of it, or began to tire of the readings Henry suggested.

Once I'd chosen science as my métier, once I'd begun my bachelor of science, I avoided those of Henry's books that were not connected to my pursuit; no novels, no poetry, and certainly no philosophy. I read only such volumes as were practical and edifying.

Edifying in theory, I mean. I don't know that a textbook on molecular biology can be called more edifying than the *Letters of Isaac Newton* (a particular favorite of Henry's), but I convinced myself it was. And I firmly closed another door between us.

Still, for many of the years before I left Henry's home, reading was an aspect of our intimacy.

From time to time over the years, especially if he hadn't seen her in a while, Henry would ask after my mother.

This was as painful for me as it must have been for him, because my mother began to see other men shortly after she moved into her own place. I inevitably disliked the men she saw and I'd say so.

— Well, Henry would answer, Mr. So and So must have his good side.

How poorly he saw my mother's flaws, or how few of them he allowed himself to admit. For instance, some of my mother's lovers were genuinely abusive. There must have been something wrong somewhere.

And, since I myself could not love her as he did, Henry's refusal to recognize my mother's defects seemed foolish.

Naturally, as I grew older, I began to speculate on Love, on Henry's love for my mother, my mother's love for wretched men, their lovelessness, my lovelessness . . . what did it all mean?

Of course, as I took my own first steps in love, I became more tolerant of Henry's blindness. Not that I understood his passion for my mother, not quite, but I found it less obscure.

I found it less obscure at sixteen, when my hormones began their treachery, but I was eighteen before I succumbed to feelings as intense, in principle, as Henry's. (Let's say I fell toward love. I don't know that I actually loved, at eighteen.)

And the experience was mystifying.

First, the self-consciousness. My clothes are tight; my clothes are loose. Are my teeth straight enough? Do my feet sweat? Why wasn't I born with more robust hair? What I wouldn't give to be loquacious, to be strong and silent. I hate my mouth. I'd look better with green eyes, better with rugged shoulders. As if Nature were a shop where I'd bought all the wrong things: narrow-chested, weak-chinned, small hands, ears like palm fronds, hair in the wrong places, hairless in the wrong places.

And then, as if that weren't excruciating enough, your mind goes off on a relentless tangent. It doesn't matter what you smell, taste, or see, it all reminds you of Lucinda (Lucinda Papadoleus). A dog's breath, in its very sourness, is a call to love. Black olives taste sweet. The moon is full and white when it's full, full and white when it isn't. And though I imagined my own body in its imperfection, hers I saw only in its radiance; the subtle curve of her nape, the graceful curve of her fingers, the delicate curve of her breasts, the precise curve of her nates.

It didn't actually matter what I experienced, nor where I experienced it. It was all wonderful.

And finally, baffled as I was, my loins entered the fray. It felt as if I were following a radiator, and that's *before* we were actually naked together, Lucinda and I. Frankly, I don't know how I ever managed erection, or coition, or ejaculation. In fact, I think I was more often provoked into one or two of the three than I was into all three in proper order.

One learns to relax, however, and I was fortunate in my partner. Lucinda was understanding and sympathetic, but the sheer variety of miscues we discovered is astounding for such a simple and, in theory, instinctive recreation.

So, I was eighteen and my affections were, inexplicably, reciprocated by Lucinda Papadoleus, herself eighteen and from Winnipeg, a city I have admired ever since. And I began to see the point of Henry's parable about Hornpayne. There were all sorts of complications in this, my first sexual relationship. And it was these that drove me to speak with Henry about love.

I assumed that he, if anyone, would be a willing guide to waters he'd obsessively sounded over the years. Instead, when I mentioned my feelings for Lucinda, Henry sighed and said

— It will pass, Tom.

The most disappointing words he ever spoke to me.

Not that he was wrong. Lucinda and I spent five months together and I spent the next six alone, recovering. It did pass, but I so resented Henry's lack of sympathy that, as far as I remember, I never mentioned my personal life again; not a word about desire or love or trust.

I wondered, bitterly, what he might have felt if, when he spoke of my mother, I sighed and answered

— It will pass, Henry.

That is, I imagined my feelings for Lucinda were commensurate with his for my mother. I didn't understand, at the time, that being young and in love, it was I who was blessed. "It will pass" was not a dismissal of the things I felt but an expression of compassion. First love dies before one realizes how extraordinary it is. It wasn't

— It will *pass*, Tom

but

— (*unfortunately*) It *will* pass, Tom (*but, if you're lucky, there will be deeper love than this*).

If I'd understood his words in this way at the time, I might have taken heart, but how could I have understood? With all the arrogance of my eighteen years, I did think myself blessed, and strong, and I was right, if "right" is what you call the almost total confusion of my strengths and weaknesses.

It was something like mistaken identity. Not knowing why I was blessed or why I was strong, not being whom I thought I was, what hope was there of knowing good fortune from misery?

It is only now, for instance, that I've begun to understand the singular dignity of Henry's passion. To be hopelessly in love with a woman who has not even rejected you, to wait in patient longing for her return, to wait without despair, keeping busy with the minute details of existence, with books, with endless experiments, maintaining an emptiness within, like sweeping a spare room, in the hope that . . . with the faith that . . .

All this I might have done, for a time, while in my twenties, or even in my thirties, if I had found the love of my life. But, to wait for decades? In one's forties, fifties, sixties? For years I thought Henry a little contemptible, but as time passed, as time passes, his waiting moves slowly, in my imagination, from contemptible to something else.

Of course, I'm assuming that I now know more about Henry, that I understand at forty a man I could not understand at eighteen, but perhaps that's assuming too much. Could it be that Henry Wing is both the ridiculous man I thought he was *and* the man who lived in loving dignity? Both? Neither?

Wouldn't it be more honest to say, now: I never really knew him, I don't understand him, yet I am deeply moved by the memory of his death.

As I mentioned, I spent hours and hours in Henry's company, often sleeping in my own room at his house (our house), though my mother had moved out and I had another home, elsewhere. And again, of these ten years, the years before I moved into a place of my own, I remember so little.

What *do* I remember?

I remember Henry asking if there were any music I enjoyed, and I said yes, there's *Revolver*—an album I'd heard, or heard of, in the years when British music was unavoidable. I'd heard of it, but the music of my time has never meant much to me.

Days later, when Henry bought *Revolver*, we sat together, respectfully listening to both sides of the album.

When it was done, he said

— It's interesting, Tom, but it sounds like keening.

I was too embarrassed to admit that, yes, it was keening, and that I'd have preferred something older, Bach, say, or da Palestrina.

I remember catching him in the act of mending his suit jackets with needle and thread.

Mending isn't always memorable, it's true, but he did it with such precision. His jackets were draped on the chairs in the dining room. Henry was in shirtsleeves. He held up the arm of a jacket and inspected it. Then, after cutting away the threads of a previous darn, he meticulously mended an elbow.

His head was so close to the fabric I feared for his eyes at each pass of the needle, but he sang softly as he darned.

And when he finished, he went on to the next jacket, and the next, inspecting mends, pulling at buttons, and so on around the table, jacket to jacket, chair to chair, in a circle.

I remember some of the names of the "manservants" Henry had over the years: Peter, Richard, David, Sylvain . . . Patrick, Arthur, Robert, Drew, Edward, Samuel.

I remember helping him with his cyclopedia or listening to him enthuse about his latest discovery: occasionalism, oneirography, Nicolas of Cusa's *interminatum* . . .

And I remember the moments that preceded my going away.

It was in the summer of 1978. I had decided, finally, to live on my own, away from Henry and away from my mother.

It wasn't a going-away for good, you understand. I left most of my things where they were, taking only books, clothes, and Alexander, my first parrot, from Henry's house; clothes and a bed from my mother's.

I had packed my books into a dozen cardboard boxes. My clothes were in two old suitcases. Henry's manservant, Sylvain I think it was, helped me bring the heavier boxes down from the third floor, while Henry himself brought down a suitcase and Alexander in his cage.

The day was beautiful, I think. It smelled of tar outside, and inside it smelled of cabbage soup, the only thing Sylvain cooked that even vaguely approached edible. The sun was so bright, it hurt to sit in the station wagon I'd borrowed, and I was worried Alexander would bake, though we weren't going all that far, only to a basement at the corner of Lyon and Gilmour.

— Du perroquet grillé, Sylvain said. Miam miam.

When the boxes were packed away and I'd buckled the belt around Alexander's cage, I went back into the house to say good-bye.

As I came in from the sunlight, I couldn't see properly. Henry was in the foyer, waiting, but there was something amiss. He seemed uncomfortable.

— You haven't left anything you need? he asked.

— No, I answered.

— You're certain?

— Of course . . .

Henry looked unnaturally thin in his gray suit; head bowed, rubbing his glasses on the sleeve of his jacket. He looked ancient, not like Henry at all. It was as if, in walking from sun to shade, I'd crossed decades.

— See you later, Henry, I said.

He put on his glasses and we shook hands.

— I'm sorry I *wasn't* your father, Tom.

What this had to do with anything, I couldn't imagine.

— Yes, well, I don't need one, I answered.

And then, once again

— See you later.

His hand was as dry as newsprint, or perhaps mine was damp. In any case, he smiled and he was Henry again as I left.

The idea of "Father" had already begun to dissipate as I shook Henry's hand good-bye. It has almost entirely faded now, though I suppose I do feel a kind of intellectual curiosity. There are biological, historical, and perhaps even sociological questions to be resolved, but no emotional ones, not really.

— I wasn't your father, Henry said.

And I remember how he said it: softly, accent on "wasn't," his hand in mine.

Is it possible he lied? He had lied to me about the transmutation of elements, but there he'd had good reason, or at least reason. He wanted to show me that if gold were so easily made, it would be worthless; that the idea of gold is infinitely more precious than gold itself.

He *would* think so, being a connoisseur of ideas, but never mind . . .

He had no reason, that I can see, to lie about his part in my birth.

The Years with Mother

You might think, if you've read this far, that our relationship (mine and my mother's, I mean) would deteriorate over these ten years—from the accidental end of my childhood (1969) to its official passing (1978). And, for the longest time, my feelings for her were certainly adulterated, usually ambivalent; happily ambivalent, painfully ambivalent, ambivalent but optimistic, ambivalent and frightened, ambivalent and guilt-ridden.

For years I wasn't any more comfortable with her than I was with Henry; not ideal circumstances for a rapprochement.

And yet . . .

One of the best things about my mother's later life was that, though she loved Henry, she thought herself happier away from him, and she seemed more at ease with smaller doses of his affection.

She had that luxury. Nothing she did spoiled Henry's feelings for her. She saw him as often or as little as she liked, for supper, for brunch on Sundays, to discuss my problems at school, to ask if I might stay with him when she was sent on one of her dreary government-sponsored courses in Chicoutimi or Trois-Rivières or Rouyn-Noranda . . .

I say she *thought* herself happy and *seemed* at ease. Ease and contentment aren't the states I associate with my mother. Given her taste in men, I don't see how she could have attained them. With my mother, I always felt, no matter where we were or what we were doing, an underlying restlessness. As far as I can remember, the only moments this wasn't so were when she first sat with Henry, in silence, and on her deathbed when she was with me, again in silence.

Still, away from Henry she sometimes behaved as if she were unburdened and, it seems to me, she developed a sense of humor.

It's possible, of course, that her sense of humor was constant and that it was I who learned to appreciate it. That would be just like my mother, constant in the most mercurial of instincts; but, in my own defense, I must say she had an unusual sense of humor.

For instance, an older woman in our neighborhood owned a large black dog, a Newfoundland. The dog was intimidating but friendly, and the woman let it sniff about the streets on its own. And then, a handful of youths moved into the house beside hers. From that time on, whenever we passed the woman on the street, she'd complain about their noise, which was deafening, their language, which was foul, and their filth, which was disgusting. It was all too much for the poor woman and, besides, the youths kept a vicious dog that terrorized the neighborhood. That is, it terrorized the neighborhood until, one day, the Newfoundland seriously injured it in a fray.

We were all of us grateful.

And then, not long afterward, the Newfoundland was beaten to death, its body left on the sidewalk. The dog was almost certainly destroyed by the youths, but there were no witnesses to the killing.

You can imagine the older woman's despair.

Anyway, we were speaking of the incident at supper one night, my mother and I, both of us horrified by the dog's death. Distracted, she pushed my supper onto my plate and, distracted, I looked down to see what it was. (It didn't usually pay to look.)

— What's this? I asked.

It was something charred, smothered in cream of mushroom. And my mother answered

— I didn't want the poor dog to go to waste, Thomas.

For a second, I almost believed her. She'd spoken so softly, so feelingly.

It says much about my younger self that I believed, however fleetingly, my mother had collected the dog's body, skinned it, and served it in Campbell's cream of mushroom. (It says as much about her cooking.)

Although I was put off my food, I laughed. We both did. We

laughed together, though it was odd to hold such conflicting images in my imagination: the dog's blood-spattered body on the pavement and, at the same time, my mother desperately trying to skin the animal for supper.

We were neither of us able to eat our pork in mushroom sauce, nor the mint jelly she served with it.

This wasn't the first time we'd laughed together, but it sticks in memory for several reasons:

- the sound of my mother's laughter
- the sensuous details (to this day, I can't stand cream of mushroom).

This was also the first inkling I had that there was more to my mother than my resentment allowed me to see; a crucial moment in our relationship.

One of the most striking differences between myself as a child and myself now is the discovery that my mother was an amusing woman. It raises all sorts of questions. I mean, I wonder how much of what I took to be distance and lack of affection was actually distance and humor? Are distance and humor preferable in a parent? Are "lack of affection" and a "sense of humor" mutually exclusive? Perhaps there was no distance at all . . . ? Perhaps it was all humor . . . ?

Of course, where humor's concerned, I'm far from expert. For most of my childhood, I was too serious to laugh at myself, too serious to laugh at much of anything. I've made up for it since. There's very little I find as hilarious as myself, I can tell you.

My mother laughed at me quite a bit, now that I think of it, but she laughed at herself as well. Perhaps laugh isn't the best word. She didn't so much laugh . . . It was rather that she couldn't take her own darkness all that seriously.

She even managed to find humor in her relationship with Gerald Perry, the only man I ever saw strike her. Him I remember exactly: tall, overweight, and blond. He never took off his leather jacket, and he smelled of motor oil.

— The fuck you lookin' at?

he asked me before pushing her against a wall and stomping out of the apartment in a rage. (Even at the time I thought I was dreaming.)

Of him, she said

— Cost me a fortune in makeup

and

— He was a good man, sweetheart. He only ever hit me on this side of the face, you know.

Her words upset me at the time, but it wasn't Gerald Perry she treated lightly, it was herself. She was her own object of ridicule, or she was at times.

It's in this that I feel closest to her.

It must seem odd, my going on about my mother's sense of humor, but, aside from bringing us gradually closer, it was like her shadow in later years.

More than a shadow.

It was after I accepted this aspect of her that she began her subtle change from Katarina to Mother, or from Mother to Katarina, depending. I mean, if mothers are autocratic and frightening, then she was my mother first. If they are loving and kind, she was most a mother just before she died.

I realize mothers are *both/and*—both frightening and loving— but I think of her kinder self as Mother, and it is disconcerting to have less vivid memories of my mother as Mother than I do of my mother as Katarina.

There is a moment that stands out, though, a moment on the cusp of Motherhood.

It was before I left my two homes, the beginning of my second year at the university: 1977.

I was twenty.

We were meeting for lunch, my mother and I, somewhere around Tunney's Pasture; the name stays with me, the neighborhood doesn't. We almost never met during the day, so I would have resented the break in my routine.

I don't remember why we had lunch together, but we were talking about Erwin Lewis, a Jamaican whose accent I never managed to decipher, the latest man to disappoint her, though he'd been on the scene a long time, it seemed to me. Eight months? A year?

The cafeteria where we ate is white in my memory; white walls, white-tiled floor. Perhaps it was winter. No, even the trays are white, and the fluorescent lights were unusually bright. Perhaps I was on the verge of illness.

My mother was wearing glasses, which she never did at home. She was dressed in a navy-blue jacket, a canary-yellow blouse, a narrow navy skirt, a pearlish necklace. She looked more like a matron when she went off to work, but less motherly.

Her hair was short, with very little gray. Her face was still smooth, no crow's-feet, save when she scowled. Her lipstick was, as it always was, too vibrant. It looked as if her lips hovered about her mouth, but aside from that she was a beautiful woman.

I don't remember how Erwin came up. How long had he been gone? Why had he left? How could he be so cruel? It all struck me as pointless.

— Why do you get involved with men like that? I asked.

— What should I do? she asked, smiling.

— You should be sensible. The way it looks to me, you like being miserable . . .

(That was a good one.)

— I don't have any sympathy for you, I said.

And I told her why. She hated herself. She was irresponsible. She lacked consideration. Moved by my own rhetoric, I made a variety of suggestions, from psychoanalysis (for her) to self-restraint. And it seemed to me we were finally communicating, that I was telling her things she hadn't heard.

I didn't believe in psychoanalysis then. I don't believe in it now. It's no more a science than testicle scratching, but I suggested it because it sounded adult, and I remember talking on and on, looking up to see her smiling face, taking her smile for encouragement.

And then I looked up and she was crying. How long had she been crying?

— Did I say something wrong?

— No, Thomas . . . I'm sorry.

She took a handkerchief from the sleeve of her jacket, took off her glasses to wipe her eyes.

— I thought you didn't love Erwin?

— But I don't . . .

— Why can't you be honest?

(Another good one.)

— What are you crying about?

— I don't know.

That put an end to the conversation. Her eyes were puffed up, her hands unsteady. Sniffling, she rooted in her purse for a compact mirror and makeup. She was thirty-nine, younger than I am now, but she seemed impossibly old.

And I was resentful, at first, because I thought: This has something to do with me . . . but I was only trying to be helpful. It's her fault for being so sensitive. She didn't have the right to take my words so seriously. She's never done that before.

It was as if she'd betrayed me.

And then I was resentful, because I thought: This has nothing to do with my words. She misses Erwin, the silly woman. She hasn't taken me seriously at all. As if it were wrong *not* to take me seriously. Did she listen to me at all? Had she ever?

Yet, in those moments, wiping her eyes and fixing her makeup, she was what she had never been to me: fully human, not at all divine.

Really, these contradictions are typical of my feelings for Mother. Where my mother is concerned, it's as if I had evolved a loving relationship with chaos.

I mean, as far as order is concerned, it seems to be true that I slipped from my mother's womb, from that particular womb, some time on January 15th, 1957. It follows, from what I've been taught, that she, Katarina MacMillan, provided half of the elements necessary for my existence.

So, of the woman who whelped me, I know a name, a date of birth, something of her parentage, and a handful of incidents from her life. Essentially, I don't know her that much more than I know my father, and the things I do know are almost useless where knowing is concerned. I mean, I can barely scratch the surface of "Who was your mother?"

Mind you, I can barely scratch the surface of "Who am I?" either.

Know thyself? Pardon my language, but the ancient Greeks should bugger off. Knowing so little of my origin, of my parents, of anything at all, how much chance is there of knowing myself? Besides, who I am is a function of when I am, and when I am is only a near fact, as evanescent as breath on a windowpane.

Yes, yes. It's the old story. Human ignorance is as common as dirt, and if I could take comfort in my ignorance, I'd be better off.

But although it has brought no comfort, ignorance has brought the only lasting passion I've known, not only a passion to know but a passion for things in place, and things in place is connection, and connection is love, or next door to it, as far as I can tell.

I'm sorry, what I mean to say is, being who I am, I might have loved my mother less if I'd known her better. My ignorance is the generator of our intimacy.

I'm not obsessed with my mother, but, as it happens, she has been the most unpredictable element in my life, the one to whom I've most often sought connection; for love, yes, but for self-protection as well.

I wonder if this makes any sense at all?

The day I moved into my apartment at Gilmour and Lyon, I invited my mother to supper.

I had no table and only two chairs.

It had taken no time at all to unpack my belongings. My books were neatly piled against the bedroom wall. My bed was covered with the only sheets I owned. The sheets were white, too small for the frame. My clothes were in a squat chest of drawers.

My kitchen utensils, or such as I had, were in a drawer I'd lined with waxed paper. They were in the same drawer as my four knives, three forks, and half a dozen spoons. There was only one kitchen cupboard, so it was just as well I had only three cups, four plates, two pots, and a frying pan.

The apartment smelled dank and earthy, though here and there it also smelled of the pine paneling the landlord had nailed to one wall. The floors were concrete and cold. There were only two windows, one in the kitchen and one in the front room, both of them such small, grimy rectangles there would have been little light from either, even if they had been higher than ground level.

The previous tenant had left a lamp, a circular rug whose black tassels made it look like a colorful insect, and a small black-and-white television that worked erratically, sometimes giving only an intimate blue light and scratchy sound.

I thought it was home and I was happy in it.

The first meal I made, in this my first apartment, was corned beef and cabbage with white rice. It must have been pretty miserable. I fried the corned beef to mush, filled the frying pan with water, added gouts of ketchup and a dose of Worcestershire sauce. I emptied a tin of corn over the beef and put a layer of cabbage on top of that.

When it had boiled into submission, I put this food-for-the-toothless on a bed of rice, and my mother and I, plates on our knees, ate in my front room.

— It's good, she said.

Even so, she only managed a mouthful or two.

— Are you sure it's all right?

— It's very good.

— Why aren't you eating?

— I want to live, sweetheart.

I couldn't hide my disappointment.

— I thought you liked it.

— I do like it, Thomas, but I'm not hungry.

She set her plate down and came over to put her arm around my shoulders.

— I don't remember the last time anyone cooked for me, she said.

— What about Henry?

— Except Henry.

She kissed my forehead.

And it occurs to me, having written so much about knowing and unknowing, having spent so much time remembering her difficult behavior, her flaws, her indecisions . . . it occurs to me again that my mother was, often, an affectionate woman.

Over the years, she was more loving than not.

(I'm wary of giving her nobility in retrospect. Her two years with Henry were, as far as I know, the only years of home and happiness she ever managed, but, it seems to me now, she fought her own destiny for them. I mean, she was, essentially, a restless woman. She must have loved Henry very much to manage even that small life with him.)

I'm tempted to write "she changed" or "I changed" or "we changed," but it's all so pointless. When do we not change? When do we stop?

She is changing now, though she's been dead for months.

As if death were a vernal state.

Housecleaning

XIII

Time passed as it usually does, not moment to moment but crest to crest.

From 1979 to 1990, things happened around me more than they did to me: Quebec squirmed and stayed, the Constitution was signed on a windy day when I was home and feverish, Clark and Turner made wonderful prime ministers, Meech Lake died, Charlottetown died; ethnic cleansing, the preservation of democracy, fatwa and jihad . . . so many interesting ways to say death, and then Death itself: buses fell from mountains, trains from bridges, planes from the air . . .

All of this I learned first from the *Citizen*, my necessary, distracting window on the world outside.

There was more, of course. There were Ilya Prigogine, Kenichi Fukui, and John Polanyi; Subrahmanyan Chandrasekhar, Carlo Rubbia, and Simon van der Meer . . .

I fell in love, I think, and out again.

Two of my toes were crushed on a Canada Day. My thumb was broken playing softball.

I moved from Gilmour to Percy, to MacLaren, to Percy.

I fell in love, I'm sure of it, and out again.

What began as summer employment, a negligible position at

Lamarck Labs, became my life, professionally speaking. From my graduation in 1979 (bachelor of science, University of Ottawa, summa cum laude, despite myself), I began to work full-time at Lamarck. I slowly progressed from observing blood tests and cell counts to helping others observe them and, finally, to supervising those who observed; not a great change in what I do, but a change in status.

It's a matter of temperament and inclination, I suppose. I like the environment. I'm as charmed by the centrifuge now as I was when I locked my first vial in. I liked looking into the refrigerators in which things were neatly arranged and labeled. The lab, with its various rooms all kept relatively clean, was hospitable to me.

Also, I liked the people with whom I worked: Linda Graham and Ron Webb, John McCann and Linda Mitchell.

I miss them.

These last twelve months, from my mother's death to now, are the longest I've been away from Lamarck since I was twenty-one, and I've begun to dream of centrifuges and plasma.

I remember so little of the years between '79 and '90, it's as though they were lived for me.

I rarely visited Henry or my mother, having other things to do, things so unmemorable they've left little, save the occasional memory of this or that pleasure, this or that distress.

And then, in 1990, my mother returned to Petrolia.

It's a decision as bewildering to me now as it was seven years ago. She had paid for a small house in Sandy Hill. She wasn't all that fond of other women, but she had, I think, a handful of friends. Whenever I saw her, she seemed content.

It would have taken more imagination than I possess to predict her return to such an unhappy town.

— I thought you liked Ottawa, I said.

— I've never liked Ottawa, she answered.

That in itself was bewildering.

She wouldn't, or couldn't, say why, but she decided to return to her parents' home.

(Now *that* was a place I thought she despised, and I was astonished to learn she hadn't sold it.)

I don't remember if I helped her pack up, or if I helped her move. I must have. Henry certainly did and, in the years of her self-imposed exile from Ottawa (or her return to Petrolia), he often asked about her well-being.

— Is she all right?

— Does she have money?

He assumed, as anyone might, that I'd have seen her more recently than he had. I was still her son, after all. And, honestly, I had every intention of visiting my mother in Petrolia. We spoke of it often.

— When are you coming to see me, Thomas?

— Soon, soon . . .

— Why don't you come this weekend? You can sleep in your old bedroom, you know.

— Well, maybe not this weekend.

To read this, it might seem as if it were my turn to punish her with solitude in Petrolia, as if I'd carried my resentment through the years. Nothing could be further from the truth. To begin with, I was thirty-three when my mother returned to Petrolia. With time, I'd managed to bury most of my grievances. And then, she was not lonely. As I understood it, she had her own life in Petrolia. She worked in Sarnia, came home to her house and friends.

And then, honestly, I intended to visit.

Yet, I never visited, not once before her final week.

You understand, I didn't realize she was dying; dying faster than usual, I mean. If I'd known . . .

If I'd known, I'd almost certainly have gone.

I lost touch with my mother, to an extent, but I lost touch with Henry too, though we lived in the same city and saw each other occasionally.

And then, a late-blooming obsession of Henry's brought us closer before pushing us even further apart.

In the spring of '95, he began a frantic and, to me, pointless search through his library. He called me at work.

— Tom, he said. I need you.

— Is everything okay?

— With me? Never better.

— What's wrong, then?

— I need your eyes.

I wondered at being asked for my eyes, but, of course, it wasn't unusual for Henry to have unusual ideas.

— Okay, then. I'll be over tomorrow.

— Tonight, he said. Please?

I've mentioned that I didn't often visit Henry once I'd found a place of my own. We spoke on the telephone. We spoke at irregular intervals, but, really, nothing could have prepared me for this Henry or for the state of our house.

It was evening. There was snow on the ground and the trees were still leafless. I had walked from Main and Hazel, along Elgin. Seventy-seven Cooper was dark, save for the lights in the library and the sitting room. When I knocked at the door, Henry answered.

— Come in, come in, he said.

But once I crossed the threshold, I didn't know where to step or where to look. There were heaps of books against the walls. There were books on the steps of the staircase; most of these were open. There were books in the middle of the floor. In the sitting room, there were books on the sofa, under the sofa, by the fireplace, on the mantel. It was as if a tornado had recently touched the library.

The only things unencumbered by books were the bookshelves. There was a path through the books, it's true, but the front of the house was almost unnavigable.

And then, to the walls, Henry had pinned hundreds and hundreds of pages. On some of these, he'd underlined a sentence or a phrase, a number or an equation. Around others he'd drawn circles in yellow chalk. On others still, he'd written messages to himself in black ink.

Henry himself was as thin as ever, but he now seemed helplessly bowed.

— What happened? I asked.

— I'm so glad you could come, Tom. I'm looking for something by Ramón Lull. I know it's here somewhere . . .

I admit that, once I'd overcome my surprise at the disarray, I was annoyed that he'd called me to find an obscure book lost somewhere in among the other obscurities. He didn't know where the book might be. He didn't know the book's name and, actually, he wasn't certain it had been written by Ramón Lull. If it came to that, we might be looking for something *about* Mr. Lull and, once we found it, its importance could as easily be in what it led to as in what it contained.

— I know it's here, though, Henry said.

Which didn't help at all.

— Do you really need it this minute?

— Oh, Tom. You know I wouldn't disturb you unless . . .

— What's it for? I asked.

— To cure cancer, he answered.

— Cancer? When did you hear you had . . . ?

Henry smiled.

— I don't have, he answered.

It was one of those moments when reality seems a fragile thing indeed. I'd been summoned to the home of a sixty-eight-year-old man and asked to help find a book by or about a certain Ramón Lull in among the heaps of books scattered throughout a three-story house.

I began to wonder how it had escaped my notice that Henry was insane.

— Why didn't you ask Samuel to help?

— Samuel's gone, Henry answered.

And, I must say, that didn't reassure me about the state of his mind.

What calmed me, and almost mitigated my annoyance, was Henry's demeanor. It's an odd thing to say, but, after all this time, he was still Henry, and the longer I looked at the old man before me, the more it struck me that this request wasn't any more peculiar than others he'd made. There was a disconcerting edge to him on this evening in 1995, but, as I followed him into the library, it was a little like following him into the lab for the first time.

And it was reassuring to know that what I'd taken for disarray was, in fact, ordered. It was a relief to learn that

a) books placed against a wall were not useful
b) books in the center of a room might, or might not, be of use, depending on the room in which they were found: those in the library being most important to his purpose; those in the kitchen, least important

c) books left open on a stairwell were awaiting judgment, or had received only cursory inspection

d) pages pinned to a wall were from books in the library

e) pages circled with chalk were of immediate interest, containing direct references to Lull

f) pages containing formulae or equations were of moderate interest

g) pages on which he'd written words or phrases were of little to no interest, but they were "suggestive."

And so on . . .

The relief I felt had nothing to do with Henry's project. I didn't believe there was a cure for cancer hidden in this particular library. It was rather that, having imposed a system to his search, Henry demonstrated clarity of mind. Still . . .

— Why do you need me? I asked.

— I need you to read the footnotes in some of the older books, Tom. My eyesight . . .

I followed him to the library. He turned on another lamp and pointed to the *Life of Marcellus Stellatus Palingenius* by Pier Angelo Manzolli. A number of pages had already been cut from the book; a straight razor lay on the table beside it.

— I'm sorry, Tommy. I can't read these footnotes at all.

He sounded almost as perplexed as I was.

— Don't you have a magnifying glass?

— I do, I do, but it hurts to use it.

There was no riposte to that.

— Maybe you could start here? he said.

I don't know if I can do justice to this evening with Henry. Its meaning alters whenever I think on it. I do know, however, that the evening is more touching in retrospect than it was at the time.

I was annoyed with Henry for disrupting my routine, for asking me to read the footnotes in a book that, as it turned out, had nothing to do with cures or Lull. I read him the bits of Latin, Italian, and English, but I did it without enthusiasm.

What was the point of this frenzied search? Was this just another of Henry's extravagant ideas?

And yet, as I read Manzolli's footnotes, looking up occasionally to see if Henry was listening, waiting as he made his own notes, I began to feel pity for him. Yes he was thin, and yes he was bowed, but it was particularly upsetting to watch his efforts to sit still and write.

We were in the library. Henry sat in the armchair and I sat across from him in a chair beneath a floor lamp. Henry was deep in the mouth of the armchair, so engulfed in his suit he looked womanish. He had a notebook on his lap and in his hand a fountain pen. His hands had curled in on themselves, like snails, and it was clearly painful for him to write. At times his hand shook so much I thought the pen would fall.

— Go on, Tom. I'm listening.

— Yes, Henry . . .

On this evening in March, leaning over the thought fragments of a man long dead, reading foreign words to a man I loved, I felt a confusion of pity and contempt.

I couldn't stand to see Henry this way: ill at ease in his own body, not at all divine.

In the months that followed, Henry often called me to read for him or, when he thought he'd discovered a possible cure, to help set up the lab for his experiments. For a time, it was black helle-bore mixed with a certain something that held the key. For a time it was stinking hellebore, then green hellebore, then not hellebore at all but motherwort mixed with something and something or something else.

He needed my assistance to set up beakers, alembics, and burners, to time reactions, to keep the laboratory spotless.

He needed my assistance to make the compounds, infusions, and poultices he administered to the rats he bought from the university.

He needed my assistance and understanding.

And what was there to inspire understanding? The cure for an infirmity in footnotes on the zodiac? A desperate hope in hellebore, motherwort, pipsissewa, spurge, and stoneroot? An eccentric old man who has pinned hundreds of pages to the walls of his home?

There was nothing in any of that to inspire confidence.

For months I was with him often, reading and assisting, but after that I found reasons to avoid what had come to seem an embarrassing duty. I answered the telephone, when I answered at all, as if I were just on my way out, on my way to somewhere so important I couldn't talk to him for long.

— Sorry, Henry.

— Not to worry, Tom.

I saw him less and less.

And, of course, when I met you (5 March 1996, almost a year after Henry began looking for Ramón Lull), my thoughts were elsewhere.

On September 1st, 1996, three days before I left to see my mother, I visited Henry to give him news of Katarina's health, to tell him, in effect, that she was not doing well, though I didn't yet know why.

That morning, a young man opened the front door and then

took me up to the den, where Henry was reading. The house was in the same state it had been: books everywhere, though those against the walls were now neatly stacked, and pages were pinned not only to the walls but to the banister and to the doors.

All the lights were on and the floor lamps had been moved to the center of the rooms they were in.

I pushed apart the doors to the den and, for a few moments, Henry was unaware of my presence. He sat with his back to me, a lamp on either side of his chair, his body almost bent in half over the book on his knees.

On the blackboard, there was a drawing of stars:

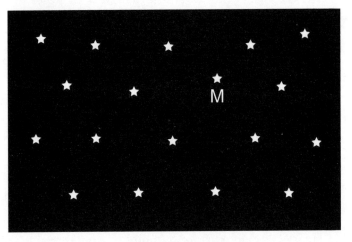

La Figure M, de Kepler

(The drawing is as mysterious to me now as it was then, but, because I assumed it was in Henry's hand, I left it on the blackboard when I came to live in this house. What wind and dust haven't obliterated is on the blackboard still. I wouldn't think of erasing it. It means something to me, the way lemon soap means, the way my gold-dust envelope means . . . whatever "M" meant to Kepler, whatever it meant to Henry, whatever it means.)

I saw the back of Henry's neck. The sinews made a soft canyon. His gray hair prickly and sparse. In one hand he held a magnifying glass close to the page of a book he held open with the other, both hands all knuckle. His lips moved as he read, but, otherwise, he was quite still.

— Henry, I said.

He looked up and turned toward me, smiling.

— Tom, he said

as if I hadn't been avoiding him for months.

— Have you come to visit?

— No, I answered. I'm on my way to Petrolia. My mother's ill.

— And you've come to tell me.

He put his book aside and, awkwardly, stood up.

— Let me make you some tea, he said.

I was about to refuse when he put his arm in mine.

— It seems like yesterday that you and Kata came to me . . . Did I ever tell you how much you resemble your mother?

— No, you never did.

We went slowly down the stairs, Henry holding fast to the banister, and then slowly to the kitchen. The autumn light was warm, the house cool. He pulled the tin of orange pekoe from its shelf in the cupboard.

— Let me do that, I said.

— It's all right, Tom.

So, I sat at the kitchen table and watched him make tea. He moved as if he were doing all this for the first time, taking a pot from the stove, filling it with water, striking a wooden match and turning on the flame, putting the pot to rest on the burner.

We waited as the water boiled, and then, when it did, he let a small handful of leaves drop into the pot. The aroma of tea permeated the kitchen.

When it had steeped, Henry brought out two white porcelain

cups and a small sieve. I thought he would spill most of the tea. His hands shook as he poured it through the sieve and into the pot. Even so, there was enough for both of us.

— Thank you, Henry.

— You're welcome, Tom.

We didn't talk about my mother. Henry wouldn't.

— My mother's ill, I said.

— So you've told me, he answered.

And that was it.

He spoke of books he was anxious to have, most of them obscure even by Henry's standards. He spoke of the plants he hoped to receive from overseas, from Alexandria, from Dakar, from Umm Qasr . . .

I didn't really pay attention to him. I thought it strange that he should speak of plants when my mother was ill.

— I have to go, I said as soon as I'd finished my tea.

— Please, come and see me as soon as you get back, please?

— Of course.

At the front door I turned to shake his hand, but I had walked ahead so quickly I had to wait for him on the doorstep. Henry put his hand on my shoulder. Not knowing what else to do, I put my arms around him. It was like embracing a sack of sticks.

— See you soon, he said.

I could see he was upset, but I didn't understand why exactly. He let me go and went back into the house, muttering

— Where did I leave the mortar

as the door closed behind him.

I left Ottawa in a rental car, the car radio for company.

I left early, in the rainfall, and arrived before evening.

Petrolia, the town itself, had changed, but only in this world. In my mind it was scarcely different, and I felt a certain nostalgia for it.

I didn't feel that way for long, you understand, but I was surprised I felt it at all. I walked along the main street, going out of my way to pass the post office and, from there, the places I'd known. I couldn't have gotten lost if I'd tried.

Grove Street was not quite as I remembered it, but I'd have had a time telling you exactly what had changed. I suppose the houses were a little more decrepit, but the field in which I'd picked dandelions was still a field, and that in itself was remarkable.

My grandmother's house and the houses around it were now my mother's house and the houses of people I didn't know.

Mr. Goodman still lived in the Goodman house, but he wasn't the man I'd feared in childhood. On my second day in Petrolia, my mother fitfully sleeping in her mother's bed, I went out for a walk. I heard my name called and there he was, standing unsteadily on his own front steps, motioning me toward him.

— Tom . . . Tom . . .

And when I approached

— Good to see you, boy, good to see you.

He tried to embrace me, but I stepped away. He stumbled.

— My legs are givin' out, he said. No feeling in 'em at all most days . . . but it's good to see you, boy . . . recognized you right away.

His hair was white. He was fat, his stomach like three pillows in a pillowcase. His face was puffed and ruddy, either from exertion or from drink.

— It's good to see you, Tom . . .

— Thank you, I said.

— Hasn't been the same since you kids left home.

— How's Mrs. Goodman? I asked.

— Mrs. Goodman? I been on my own for goin' on ten years.

— I'm sorry.

— Nothin' to be sorry for, 'less you were the bitch she left with.

He was suddenly angry.

If it had been anyone else, I'd have walked away without another word, but Mr. Goodman was still an adult to me. He was still Margaret's father. The respect I showed him was involuntary.

— I have to leave now, I said.

— Your mother's sick, is she? he asked.

— Yes.

— You're a good boy, Tom. None of my own ever visit.

He was suddenly sad.

— Come over for a drink with the old man, he said. I'll call the girls.

— Maybe tomorrow, I answered.

Though I knew I would not return to that house, to that basement, Margaret or no.

So, Grove Street had scarcely changed, and my grandmother's house was so much my grandmother's house, I startled at the sight of it.

I knocked, but the front door was open.

The living room was dim, but the house wasn't quiet.

— Hello?

I could hear my mother's voice, and then a man's voice.

— Hold her for me, please.

I went up the steps and pushed on the door to Grandmother's bedroom. My mother was on the bed, held by a woman in white as a man withdrew a syringe from her thigh. I knew, of course, that these were a doctor and a nurse, that they were seeing to my mother. For a moment, though, it was as if I'd discovered a shameful intimacy.

The doctor turned to me.

— And you are? he asked, not unkindly.

— I'm Katarina's son, I answered.

— Lorraine, will you clean up for me?

— Yes, doctor.

And again, to me

— Could you come with me for a minute?

— What's going on? I asked.

The doctor, a light-skinned black man, some six feet tall, with short hair and a gaunt face, looked at me with surprise and a sort of disappointment.

— Your mother's dying, he said.

— I thought she was sick.

— Of course she is. She has cancer.

— Cancer?

You can imagine my state of mind, or perhaps not.

I discovered my mother was dying so soon before her death. The morphine the doctor had given was, more or less, an admission of defeat. They'd known for months she was going to die, but a milder drug had taken care of both pain and inflammation. It wasn't doing a thing by the time I got there, and that was a presage of the end.

And then, that she should be dying of the thing for which Henry had so idiosyncratically sought a cure.

My mother herself had been silent on the matter. To what purpose? To hide what from whom? It occurs to me now that she'd called me more often than usual that summer, but I'd carried on as if . . . promising to visit when . . . blissfully unaware of . . .

So, when the doctor said

237

— She has cancer

I was confused.

— Cancer?

— Yes. It sounds as if you didn't know.

In the days that followed, I had time to meditate on what I didn't know.

We were not alone, my mother and I, though the house was quiet. The house was quiet and, during the day, most of the lights were off, so as not to disturb her sleep. My mother never again left her room, but her nurse, a cheerful, big-boned woman, insisted that there be soft light at all times, in all rooms, if possible.

— Ohh, Mr. MacMillan, it's so much better to go out like we come in.

Meaning what, I wondered, though I had no use for bright light, anyway. It wasn't as if I wanted to read, and when I needed respite from my deathwatch, I went outside and walked around. She herself, the nurse I mean, kept the house tidy, saw to my mother's needs, and, when she wasn't at her duties, read in the kitchen, by lamplight: *The Chamber*.

And my mother . . .

My mother was as thin as my grandmother, her hair damp and white. The cancer, which began in her breast, was now so deep it had invaded her bones. She had broken an arm while turning in her sleep. It was better for her to lie still.

For the most part, she slept, and I sat in an armchair beside her watching her struggle with the white top sheet, as if the sheet itself were her tormentor. From time to time, when she was awake and knew I was there, I held her hand, but I was so worried I'd break her bones, it gave me no comfort, whatever comfort it gave her.

Though it was as much the dim light as the change in her appearance, it was disconcerting to see Edna in Katarina. I recognized my own mother by her eyes, her nose, her forehead, and her ears. It was in these small things she was my mother.

I was not always myself for her, either. She called me "Father," and "Henry," and, once, "Mother." (It's odd to think that, in the two of us, briefly, two versions of my grandmother held hands before whatever it is that Death is.)

Not that we didn't speak in the two days we had together, she as herself, myself as Thomas. We did, but not much. Or, I should say, the moments during which we used words were brief. We spoke without them, or without exchanging them.

At times she was

aware of my presence, smiling

aware of my presence, unsure of who I was

aware of my presence, smiling, unsure where we were.

And I would speak.

— I'm here, Mother . . .

— It's Thomas . . .

— We're in Petrolia . . .

And the nurse, on her side of the bed, with gentle authority

— Your mother needs her rest, Mr. MacMillan.

— She mustn't exert herself.

— Your mother needs . . .

And my mother, once, softly

— Thomas . . . who is that bitch?

— It's your nurse, Mother.

And the nurse

— I'm so sorry, Mrs. MacMillan. You want to be alone with your son.

And she left us alone.

You would think, these being our last moments together, that my mother and I would speak of essential things. I've never had any luck with essential things, though. Besides, neither of us knew these were our last moments. We spoke about the weather, about the drapes, about the bedsheets, and finally

— Are you comfortable?

— Is it night?

— Not quite yet.

— Where's Henry?

— He's in Ottawa.

— I missed you, Thomas.

— I missed you too.

— Is Henry with you?

— He's not here . . .

And then, on the verge of sleep

— Did he tell you . . . ?

— Henry?

— I'm tired, sweetheart . . .

And it occurred to me to say

— Wait . . .

thinking there was something I meant to say, something like

— Wait, I want to . . .

or

— Wait, I haven't told you . . .

but, unable to discover what else I wanted to say, I said

— Sleep, Mother.

So my last words to her were as unrevealing as hers were to me.

I might have asked about my father.

At the time, however, my father's identity was not in my thoughts. I was concerned for my mother. I wondered if she was comfortable, if the light was painful to her, if there were not enough light, if the bed had always been this small . . .

My father?

I am, I think, Henry's son, whoever fathered me, and yet . . .

My father, given that I had one, would have resembled Mr. Mataf much more than he did Henry.

Mr. Mataf was the archetypal man in my mother's life. All the others, save Henry, were variations on him, some taller, some shorter, some more violent, some less resourceful.

(Of course, it's unlikely Mr. Mataf actually was my father. For one thing, my mother was not constant. It's difficult to believe she'd have maintained a relationship with any man from the year of my birth to the year she returned for me, from 1957 to 1967. For another, if Mr. Mataf had known I was his son, he'd have behaved differently, I think, not just where I was concerned, but in general.)

For Henry to have been my father, my mother would have to have met him, at the very latest, in 1956.

There's nothing improbable in that, but is it possible Henry knew he was my father and kept it from me?

Why would they have withheld this for thirty years?

What reason could there be for such stubborn silence?

No, I don't think Henry was my father. Henry was among my mother's final thoughts, that's all, and that was less surprising to me than the tone of her voice. It was sad to hear her ask

— Where's Henry?

It was she who left him, after all. Had she wished it, he'd have been with her then, or she with him.

What to make of a woman whose life was spent loving men with whom she couldn't stay?

From the moment I said
— Sleep, Mother
the room was quiet.

Outside it was early afternoon and bright. The streets were childless. It was late summer. I walked through town: toward Reeces Corners, back again toward Oil City, over to the golf course and the tile factory . . .

A long walk through a town that was neither mine nor, as yet, not-mine. I kept my head down, to avoid familiar buildings or faces, looking up only to admire the trees along the road.

I returned when it was evening and dark for true.

The streetlamps were on, as were the lights in my mother's living room. The front door was open.

In the kitchen, Dr. Attale, the same man who'd greeted me on my arrival, was speaking to my mother's nurse.

— Her last was . . . ?

And, seeing me

— Mr. MacMillan, my condolences. Your mother has died.

I noticed the initials on his black bag (H. C.) and the white of the nurse's socks.

They were looking for something erratic in my behavior, both of them, but I have rarely felt so stable.

— Thank you, I said.

I went to the bedroom, because it seemed the thing to do. The nurse had brushed my mother's hair, straightened the room, and opened the curtains. It was night and a lamp was on.

My mother's eyes were closed. I stifled the impulse to open them.

The bedsheet was pulled up to her chin.

Despite myself, I bent down and kissed her forehead and though I felt a great many things, I managed to throttle my emotions.

My mother died at 58 years, 7 months, 23 days.

She was buried three days later, on a Tuesday.

There was a small number of people at her funeral. I knew none of them, save for Irene Schwartz.

— I'm sorry about your mother, she said.

She'd come to see me as much as she'd come to pay her respects to Katarina. Irene held my hand and brushed her cheek against mine. Her skin was dry.

— How is your mother? I asked.

— You know, Mother lives in Minneapolis now.

— I didn't know, I said.

And, for a moment, I was saddened at the thought I might not see Mrs. Schwartz again.

— I'll tell her about your mother.

We sat through the service, Irene and I. We went together to the graveyard and watched my mother's coffin lowered into the same ground that held my grandmother and grandfather.

(It will never hold me.)

When the coffin had settled and the priest turned away, Irene said

— Come visit us, Tom. My husband would love to meet you.

— Of course.

— My daughter looks so much like Mother . . . You must visit.

— Of course, I said
though I never did.

The days immediately following my mother's death, and before her burial, were among the most tranquil I have known.

It's true I had to contend with my mother's lawyer, a man who kept me in his office for an hour before reading her simple will.

And then, the day after my mother's body was carried away, I made arrangements to sell the house:

Family Home for Sale
All Reasonable Offers Considered

My mother's house was tidy. There was nothing to clean and very little to straighten.

So, once I'd completed the business of her death, I shut myself in.

My mother had accumulated a cupboard full of soup; consommé, tins of beef consommé, bought on sale, I imagine, there being no logical explanation for so much of it. There were stale crackers, there was butter, and there was a jar of mint jelly. Not that it mattered to me. I was not hungry.

I wandered about the house, spending time in my old room or in the kitchen or in the living room or, at last, in my mother's bedroom. (How alarmingly easy it is, at times, to do nothing at all.)

It was painful to enter my mother's bedroom, difficult to stay, but I did stay.

For a woman who was not obviously nostalgic until her later years, my mother had preserved a good deal of her own past.

As in my grandmother's time, a mirror hung above the chest of drawers. My grandparents still looked out from their silver frame. The room no longer smelled of lavender, but the bookshelves were filled with the same schoolbooks, hymnals, and books for children.

And yet, none of these things, the bookshelves, the hymnals, or the chest of drawers, was as perplexing to me as her letters, still where I'd found them thirty years before, but now in among my mother's things.

You understand, it wasn't the letters that confused me. I'd read them already; without much understanding, it's true, but, still, their content wasn't entirely unexpected. Rather, I found it sad that she'd kept mementos of her time in the wilderness. It must have pained her to read them.

> *Dear Mother,*
>
> *I'm so grateful you can keep Thomas a little longer. I miss him so much. I really wish you could send me a picture of him, but I don't know how much longer I'll be in Saskatoon and I don't know where we're going from here.*
>
> *You can't imagine how hard it is to be separated from your baby. I don't think you can compare it to anything else. I'll be coming back for him as soon as I find work. I know some people who have a car. We'll drive back for Thomas as soon as I find work.*
>
> *I'll write again when I have a new address.*
>
> *Bye for now,*
> *Kata*

That, written in 1961, is the first of the letters my grandmother kept. The rest, all of which I have before me now, are much the same, all promising my mother's speedy return, some asking for money. In several letters she sounds remorseful, in others resentful, hopeful, contrite . . .

The tone of the letters is much as you'd expect from a young woman who despised her mother. There are few details about her whereabouts, even fewer about the people she is with. In only one letter does she actually give an address: 77 Cooper Street, but in Vancouver.

Perhaps most disappointing is that when, in 1965, she began to write little messages to me in her letters home, they were as unrevealing as her words to my grandmother. I sometimes think it was kindness that prevented my grandmother from reading these letters to me. It would have been upsetting to hear that my mother was on the verge of return when she was not.

I don't mean to suggest that these letters were meaningless to me, that while I waited for my mother's funeral I rediscovered a few worthless, time-yellowed pages, thirty sheets in all, that I might just as easily have left behind with the other things I left behind: clothes, books, furniture, umbrellas, tins of consommé.

Nothing could be further from the truth.

While I was alone in the house, I read my mother's letters over and over, not anxiously, not even with nostalgia, but meticulously. I picked through my mother's words as Mrs. Williams used to pick through heaps of white rice to find blackened grains, or worse.

I would have liked to discover some hint of my origins, I suppose, or a vivid depiction of her struggle to return, of her state of mind.

For two days I had the letters spread out on the kitchen table; each within reach, their pages smelling of the wooden drawer where they'd been sequestered. I read them over and over until, after a while, I was as familiar with their spaces as I was with their words, and each of her words was flooded by possibilities. For instance, "Dear" and "Mother"...

"Dear Mother": That was conventional, it's true, but it was impossible to tell whether she meant "*Dear* Mother" or "Dear *Mother*" or both or neither or some combination of the two in which "Dear" attained the importance of "Mother" or moved away from it. Resentment, deep regard, love, mistrust: a host of possible emotions flowed over or settled into each word, like water on limestone. As you can imagine, if words as banal as "Dear" and "Mother" had such volutes, I had no chance with more complex words, like "grateful" and "Saskatoon." After a while, I lost the sense of *them* entirely.

For two days I spent hours in the kitchen, curtains open in the day, lights on at night, standing over my mother's letters or sitting before them, a child looking for . . .

A child looking for its mother? No, not quite that. I wasn't filled with panic or longing. I was, for the most part, calm. Still, there was a moment, late the second night, exhausted from reading . . . there was a moment when I was, briefly, overwhelmed.

I'd been looking at my mother's words for so long, they actually disappeared. It was as if bleach had fallen on the words my mother wrote. The rest of the world remained: the table, the light, the darkness outside the kitchen window.

I began to despair. I was convinced my stability was lost, when I noticed that though the words had gone, the punctuation hadn't. The almost insignificant ticks my mother had made on paper, the periods and commas, remained.

This kind of thing doesn't happen to me often, you understand, and even at the time I knew my mind was pulling my leg, but I saw the periods and commas not as punctuation but rather as the short breaths my mother had taken.

Dear Mother (breath)
 I'm so grateful you can keep Thomas a little longer (long breath) *I miss him so much* (long breath) *I really wish you could send me a picture* (breath) . . .

And it suddenly occurred to me that the little ticks that live in the carpet of a page, the periods and commas I mean, were the only precious things in her letters. They were the silences by which I'd known her for years. Had I been able to see them, I'd have erased her words myself, the better to see the punctuation.

For one ecstatic moment, somewhere near the middle of a quiet night in early September, two days after her death, I could see and hear the soft sound of my mother's breathing: through me, above me, within me.

You understand, I needed sleep.

And I fell asleep with my head on the kitchen table, the pages of my mother's letters scattered about; lights on, lights out.

This wasn't a decisive moment in my life. Nothing was revealed, nothing resolved, and, naturally, when I awakened, I could see the words my mother had written.

Still, it was something. It was the first episode of farewell, let's say. And the next morning, as I shook Irene's hand and answered

— Of course
I had no desire to see anything more of Petrolia.
I was already gone.

I left the next day: Wednesday.

I had hours to myself on the way home. Southwestern Ontario curled up behind me, like an old map.

My imagination was filled with versions of you, of my mother, and, in particular, of Henry. I scarcely noticed the landscape, though on the skirts of London, the touches of red and yellow distracted me for a kilometer or two.

Henry was first in my thoughts for a number of reasons:

1. I would have to tell him of my mother's death. (I might have told him at once, by telephone, but I'd put it off.)
2. I wanted to comfort him on the death of the woman he loved.
3. Henry was now the only person I knew whose memories of my mother somewhat coincided with my own.
4. I wondered how he'd known about my mother's cancer and why he hadn't told me.

That is, I now assumed his impassioned search for Ramón Lull was motivated by love, that his ransacking of the library was a noble eccentricity. I was sorry that I hadn't seen it that way from the beginning.

(It's not clear to me that Henry knew my mother was dying, nor that he knew he knew, but I accept that, where my mother was concerned, it was possible for Henry to know without knowing. I'm not saying I understand any of this, but I accept it. It is easier that way.)

I'd left Petrolia, in my rental car, at 11:30 in the morning. I was in Ottawa at 6:00 in the evening, as the light of day waned.

It was cold and my city smelled of wet ground.

And I was disheartened, as I walked along Cooper, to see that Henry's house was lit up, all lights on, as if for a soirée. It saddened me to be the bearer of gloomy tidings, but I pressed on.

The front door was opened by a short man in a double-breasted suit, Mr. Van Leuwen.

— Yes? he asked.

— Can I speak to Henry, please?

— No . . . that you can't do. You're late for the reception. A few of the old-timers are still here, though. Come in if you want.

— You don't understand, I said. I have very important . . .

But he had turned away from me, his right hand making circles in the direction of the sitting room.

The house was immaculate. There was not a fiber out of place. The walls were white and the panes of glass in the doors were almost invisible. If I hadn't known, I could not have guessed how recently confusion had prevailed.

In the sitting room, there were half a dozen older men, all formally dressed. Three of them sat close together on the sofa; two stood by the fireplace. On the mantel two bright-red candles burned. A third man, perhaps the eldest, sat stiffly in an armchair. This one reminded me of Henry, but I knew none of them, and there was something sinister about the gathering.

As I approached the gentlemen by the fireplace, one of them turned to me and stared.

— You're rather young, he said
and he began to blink.

— Excuse me, I said

and moved away before he could take hold of my coat.

It was at that moment that the manservant, whom I'd met a week before, entered with a platter of banana fritters. I advanced on him as if I were famished.

— Where's Henry? I asked

not quite casually.

— Mr. Wing was buried this morning, he answered.

He tried to pass by, to serve the fritters, but, in my confusion, I assumed there'd been some mistake.

— Why? I asked.

He must have thought I was joking.

— It's customary after the embalming, he said.

I'm not prone to violence, but I saw myself strangling the man; my hands around his neck, his neck in my hands.

— You're Thomas, someone said.

— Yes, I answered.

— Thomas . . . Henry died on Sunday.

The speaker, Mr. Van Leuwen, emerged from behind the man-servant.

— How? I asked.

— Coronary thrombosis while he was working. While he was working. You couldn't ask for better than that.

— Wonderful death, murmured one of the men on the sofa.

— We die like dogs, said the man in the armchair (bitterly).

— Yes, but quick is good, said Mr. Van Leuwen.

And he added

— I'm sorry I couldn't reach you sooner, Thomas. You were not at home, I think.

— No.

— Not to worry. Let me introduce you to the stragglers.

If I'd doubted these were the friends of Henry Wing, their

conversation would have convinced me. Once I'd been introduced to

Mr. Turcott (in the armchair)
Mr. . . . (by the fireplace)
Mr. . . . (by the fireplace, "rather young")
Mr. Elliot (on the sofa)
Mr. . . . (on the sofa, "wonderful death")
Mr. Chambers (on the sofa)

they began to speak, intimately, not of Henry exactly, but of the
things he adored: Federico da Montefeltro's library at Urbino,
the great library in Alexandria, the letters of Isaac Newton, the
music of Couperin, and "Katarina," whom none but Mr. Van
Leuwen had met.

I didn't know whether to remain or to go, how to remain,
how to go.

When I did leave, an hour or so after I'd arrived, I simply got
up and wandered out, leaving my coat and my suitcase behind.

Henry died at 69 years, 7 months, 24 days, only one day after
my mother.

I hope to God there are no more deaths as desolating.

It wasn't that my mother's death affected me less than
Henry's, but with Henry's passing I lost almost as much of my
mother as I did of him. I lost the light his feelings cast on her.

And, in a way, she and Henry walked into darkness together.

Henry left all of his earthly possessions, which included his
house, thousands of dollars in stocks and bonds, and the money
he had in a savings account ($78,999.88), to my mother and me.

This is my inheritance; though, of course, it is no compensation for loss, for any loss.

It was difficult, in the weeks after his death, to visit Henry's grave, but I went. I went often. His tombstone, a solid rectangle of polished black granite, is snug against the other stones and statues. His name is carved in elegant letters and, beneath it, in finer characters, are the Latin:

spatio brevi spem longam reseces

I've had time to think about those five words, but I can't decide if they mean

our span is brief; cut back great hopes

or

keep your great hopes in a small space.

The first reading is literal, but it's utterly un-Henry. I don't believe he could have curtailed his hopes for an instant. (And, of course, his greatest hope was for my mother's love.)

The second reading is wrong, but it is Henry to the letter, the grave being only a more modest place for the quality that was his essence: Hope (again, for Katarina).

So, I choose to take *spatio brevi* this second way, as love prolonged.

And yet, my doubt about the meaning of *spatio brevi* was one of the things that spurred me to write, to write this.

I mean, in February, as I brushed the snow from his tombstone, it occurred to me how typical it was that I didn't really know *what* Henry had in mind in choosing these particular words. I began to reflect on how little I'd known of his life in general. Who had his close friends been? Mr. Van Leuwen? Mr. Chambers? Why hadn't I bothered to ask?

The cemetery was deep in snow.

It was cold, but the sun was bright. The sky was blue and, in the snow, I could see the footprints of others who'd come out to visit their dead.

Was I the only one who knew so little about the deceased?

Did I know anything at all?

Can one love what one doesn't know?

Strange, isn't it, that from such small questions so much writing springs.

XIV

——

And so I've come full circle, or full spiral, or perhaps only up through the ground. (I mean, Time is the ground, but my analogy is weak.)

I am sitting in the reading room, at a large wooden desk, before a window that looks out onto the street. It is the 15th of September 1997.

It is eleven o'clock in the morning and cold.

On the desk beside me are the things I've had with me for six months. In no particular order:

> Poetry (*Norton's Anthology*)
> Letters (from Katarina to Edna)
> *Treasure Island*
> Envelope (with gold dust)
> *Della Francesca ou les ébats de l'amour*
> Key (to a lost orrery)
> Timetables (1978 to)
> *Life of Marcellus Stellatus Palingenius*
> Weeds (from Umm Qasr)

On his perch beside the bookshelves, Alexander the Second moves laterally, from one side of the crossbar to the other, and back. He's been particularly active these past few days.[10]

He senses my anxiety, I think. You'll be here tomorrow (7:00 P.M.) and, I confess, the thought is nerve-racking.

So why did I invite you at all?

Now that's a question I can answer.

There was a night, months ago. I thought it might be our last together. I parted the drapes of your bedroom window, because I couldn't sleep and I wanted to look out. I saw the corner store, the small houses, the rooftops, all of them whitened by moonlight or white with snow. And I was thinking of words for whiteness (milk, ivory, lily, chalk) when you said

— Come to bed . . .

your back to the window, your body so still it was as if you hadn't awakened to say the words.

I almost wondered if you were speaking to me.

And, again, what do you know of me?

It's as you said

---

[10] How seldom I've mentioned either of the Alexanders in all this, but how important they've been to my life. I feel blessed walking into the sitting room to lift the cowl from the cage, to hear (as I used to hear from the first Alexander)

— aaawk . . . gallop apace . . . gallop apace . . .

to hear (nowadays, from Alexander the Second)

— Dusha moya . . . aaawk . . . vyeshchaya dusha . . .

Even if they couldn't speak, my birds would be portals out. I can't look at Alexander, an African gray, without speculating about the journey he's made to me, about who it was taught him to speak.

And I can think of few days as sad as the one when the first Alexander fell from his perch, beating his wings uselessly, spinning about before dying.

I felt as helpless as a child.

— Tom, you've never asked me to your place . . .

Yet it was only then, as I stood by the window, it struck me that I'd never invited anyone home, let alone this woman whom, to my dismay, I love.

And so, these many months later, I have invited you to this home, though it is as much Henry's as it is mine.

I spent much of the morning housecleaning.

How strange it is that certain rooms, the ones I don't often visit, should become untidy.

I mean, you'd think it was my presence that brought untidiness, and, it's true, the rooms I visit often are more conspicuously untidy.

Yet even unfrequented rooms, like those in the basement and those on the third floor, need constant looking into.

Not that I'm obsessed with cleanliness. Not at all. It hardly matters to me if a room is untidy or not, because I enjoy the physical sensation of cleaning.

My bedroom, for instance.

I change the sheets. I make the bed. I sweep the room. I wipe the walls. I clean the windows with newspaper and vinegar.

Each of these things is a pleasure in itself, but it is also a pleasure to decide which to do first (change, make, sweep, wipe, or clean), to decide on an order in which to do the room.

In any case, this morning, as I was dusting, thinking of nothing in particular, I remembered an evening decades gone:

My mother and Henry were in the lab, in near darkness, the only light coming from a low, yellow flame that lit their faces from beneath. An unusually large bell jar was on the table before them, and in the jar were what I took to be two or three brown moths that fluttered and ascended before bursting into bright, white flame.

I was horrified, horrified but amazed that the moths should burn so brightly. They lit up every corner of the small room.

My mother's arm was lightly in Henry's and, looking up at the same moment, both of them smiled.

They weren't killing moths, of course. What I'd taken for insects were squares of rice paper dabbed with something and phosphorus. They fluttered and ignited when Henry let air into the jar.

I was spellbound, and it disturbed me that I'd forgotten this moment until today. I felt, for a queasy instant, as if, in these pages, I'd misrepresented myself to myself.

Have I been happier than I thought?

Well, yes and no . . .

Time, which isn't like ground at all, washes things up without regard for order or sense. My life comes back to me in various pieces, from Pablum to tombstones, each piece changing the contour of the life I've led.

I will have thousands of childhoods before time is done.

But this one has its own necessity.

Until six months ago, I didn't think it important to look back. I was content to remain closed to myself.

And then, a kind of curiosity crept in.

There was no moment in particular, no reason, or there were moments and reasons.

Last week, I put my hand on your arm as you made to cross Bank Street against the light.

— Marya, I said

and a car sped by, not two feet from us.

— What is it, Tom?

and I said

— Nothing.

Because there were no words for the confusion I felt.

Watching you step from the curb, I was myself and my mother and my grandmother.

After all, I come from somewhere.

It has form, the past, but it is distance that makes it something other than wisp. In time I shall see more clearly, and I'll begin again, another retrospect when I must.

And that is something I can do; wait, I mean.

In fact, now that I think of it, it is something I have done from my earliest days: keeping still, looking, waiting.

I once thought Henry's patience a little excessive, but I wonder if it isn't waiting that binds me to him, to a man for whom waiting was love.

I am not his equal in patience, but, you know, I believe I am able to wait, not without anxiety or sadness, but rather, like Henry, in the hope that . . . with the faith that . . .

Whatever it is time brings.

ACKNOWLEDGMENTS

Parts of this novel appeared in different form in the following journals: *Exile* and *This Magazine*.

———

The Osip Mandelshtam poem that appears on pages 44–45 is from *Stone*, copyright © 1981 by Princeton University Press, translated by Robert Tracey. Reprinted by permission of Princeton University Press.

Mr. Mataf's dialogue on page 103 is a lyric from "I Can't Help Myself (Sugar Pie Honey Bunch)" by Brian Holland, Lamont Dozier, and Edward Holland, Jr., © 1965, renewed 1993 by Jobete Music Co., Inc. All Rights Controlled and Administered by EMI Blackwood Music, Inc., (BMI) on behalf of Stone Agate Music (A Division of Jobete Music Co., Inc.). All Rights Reserved. International Copyright Secured. Used by Permission.

———

The lines in French in the epigraph are reprinted from the Jean-Joseph Rabearivelo poem *Ton oeuvre*. The English translation is provided by the author.

The lines on page 5 are from the Archibald Lampman poem *Heat*. The lines on page 7 are from the Archibald Lampman poem *September*.

The lines on page 107 are from the John Donne poem *Hymn to God My God, in Sickness*, and the lines on page 132 are from the Thomas Wyatt poem *The Long Love That in My Thought Doth Harbor*.

The passage on page 119 is adapted from *Roget's Thesaurus*, 1941 edition.

The image of Kepler's "Figure M" on page 232 is adapted from the image found in Alexandre Koyré's *Du monde clos à l'univers infini*.